BRYHER

ROMAN WALL

A NOVEL

PANTHEON BOOKS

NEW YORK

FOR

N. P

NOTES
On Place- and Other Names

ALEMANNI: Confederation of German tribes (Alle Männer), living originally along the Upper Rhine and Danube in what is now Württemberg and Baden. In the middle of the third century, they penetrated the Empire as far as Milan where they were defeated by Gallienus (258). After this, they occupied most of the land north and east of modern Switzerland, including the headwaters of the Rhine, the Saône and the Danube.

AUGUSTA RAURICA: Modern Augst, south of the Rhine near Basle. Though burned by Caesar, it was rebuilt and became a garrison town, noted for its gladiator fights.

AVENTICUM: Modern Avenches, in the Canton of Vaud, Switzerland, where remains of aqueducts, amphitheatre, many temples and wall are still to be seen. It was the main cultural and political centre of the Romans in Helvetia.

BERGOMUM: Modern Bergamo, Italy, 33 miles north-east of Milan.

BITHYNIA: Region of north-west Asia Minor, noted for its timber and agricultural products. It was willed to Rome in 74 B.C. by its last monarch, Nicomedes IV.

BRIXIA: Modern Brescia, an old Celtic town made a colony by Augustus.

CERESIO: Modern Lugano; as in modern times, the lake and the city in the Canton Ticino, Switzerland, bore the same name.

7

CROTON: Modern Crotone, on the sole of the Italian boot. As a Greek city, it was noted for its doctors and its athletes. As a Roman colony, it was somewhat less prosperous.

DACIA: Modern Transylvania, within the loop of the lower Danube. Shortly after the time of our story, it was abandoned to the Goths, following a twenty-year siege.

GENUA: Modern Genoa, one of the chief trading centres for Rome and her northern provinces.

ILLYRIA: A variable region on the eastern Adriatic, roughly comparable to modern Yugoslavia. Its tribes, never quite Romanized though they were, made it a mine of sturdy troops for the emperors of the first three centuries.

ISTER: The Danube. In its upper regions, it was one of the great natural barriers protecting the Empire.

LOUSONNA: Modern Lausanne; together with Geneva and Nyon, it guarded the strategic Roman road toward the east.

LUGDUNUM: Modern Lyons. As early as the first century, there was a gold and silver mint there. Though burned in 197, it remained an important trade and administrative centre.

MEDIOLANUM: Modern Milan. From Augustus on, the emperors made it their chief northern retreat, though none before Maximian fixed his residence there.

MINNODUNUM: Modern Moudon (German Milden) in the Canton of Vaud, between Berne and Lausanne.

MOLOSSIAN: Coming from Epirus, in north-western Greece. Wall paintings from Pompeii show country homes guarded by Molossian hounds.

NARBONENSIS: Modern Narbonne, on the River Aude,

France. Ancient authors call it a great trading centre; tin from Spain and Britain passed through the city.

NOVIODUNUM: Modern Nyon, on Lake Geneva. It was the first stop east of Geneva on the Roman road toward Argentoratum (Strasbourg).

ORBA: Modern Orbe, south-west of Lake of Neuchâtel. Third-century life there is reflected in a famous mosaic, showing a peasant and his ox-cart in a sleepy country scene.

PANNONIA: Roman province to the south and west of the Danube, north of the Drave; now western Hungary, with part of Austria. Here, as in so many provinces, the Romans traded roads for soldiers.

PENNILOCUS: Modern Villeneuve, at the eastern end of Lake Geneva.

RHAETIAN WINE: Wine from Rhaetia, west of the Helvetians, comprising modern Grisons, the Tyrol and northern Lombardy. It was the only Gallic wine not considered inferior to Italian products; writers of the early Empire follow Augustus in admiring it.

VINDONISSA: Modern Windisch, in the Canton of Aargau. From the first to the third century A.D., fortified camp of the Roman Legion, with barracks for ca. 11,000 soldiers.

I

Orba. May, A.D. 265

NENNIUS!"
There was no reply. Everything was still. Sharp
new ivy leaves climbed over the stone wall, there was a
heavy scent of grass and clover, summer was in the air,
and the villagers, working in the meadows below the
villa, were so far away that they were simply moving
dots.

"Nen-ni-us!"

"It's useless shouting like that, Valerius, you know as
well as I do that haymaking has begun."

Valerius turned quickly as his sister came out of the
kitchen on to the terrace. She had been baking, and her
arms were flecked with dough. "Where is your cook
girl, Julia?" he demanded. "I hate to see you get cinders
on your hands." With one of those flashes of memory
that seemed to occur more frequently as he got older,
he remembered her standing under an olive tree at some
family festival, the year that he had joined the army.
"Look at her grave face," his mother had exclaimed,

"she *is* a handmaid of Ceres; it isn't play to her." Julia had been the baby of the family; she was seven years younger than he was. How he had teased her during the rest of that evening, calling her a statue, and saying that stone figures needed no cakes. He smiled now as he looked up at her; she still had a calm and quiet beauty which she spoiled, he felt, by an ever growing austerity, expressed in continual toil.

"At haymaking every pair of hands is needed. I sent the girls over to the fields myself. And now, Valerius, what is it that you want? Something to eat after yesterday's journey?"

"The water isn't hot," he said, helplessly. He had never needed a bath as much as at this moment, but there was nothing in the basin but a stone dolphin, as solemn and parched as himself.

"I know. That corner pipe has cracked again. I sent Nennius over to see Scopas yesterday, but he hasn't a man to spare, they are haymaking like ourselves. You will have to wash at the fountain and then, while you have breakfast, you can tell me what happened at Aventicum. You were so late arriving last night, and so tired, that all you could say was, 'Vinodius is a fool.'"

"I could eat something," Valerius grumbled. Actually it was the bath that he had wanted most; these long rides brought out unexpected stiffnesses in the limbs. Still, if the pipe had broken, it had broken; but instead of going into the courtyard, he walked across the terrace to look down at the meadow beneath them, where swathes of purple flowers were waving, because this field was the last cut, among grasses that were almost the silver of the kitchen ashes that Julia saved to use in her own garden. At least they would have another fine day.

The Roman who had built the villa had known how to choose his site. It stood on the crest of some slightly rising ground. Below the wall, rich corn lands stretched into a plain several miles wide. Beyond this, there were woods again and hills, and on his right hand, on a clear day, Valerius could see the saddleback ridge of the snowy and terrible Alps. Lousonna lay in a line with his outstretched thumb, and if some distant trees had not been in the way, he could almost have watched the ships at anchor in its harbour.

How shocked he had been, Valerius remembered with amusement, when he had discovered on arrival that the benches were on the terrace instead of in the atrium. He was not a man who liked changes. After the first summer he had understood; no colonnade, no formal garden, could approach the splendour of the landscape before his eyes. He could smell the hay, count any whorls of the white meadow flowers that were taller than their fellows, or watch the eager dogs chasing mice as the men moved forward with their scythes.

What would the original owner say, if he could re-visit his property now? The paintings had either faded or were hanging in strips; there were several pieces missing from the calendar pavement beyond him, and two soldiers, tugging as one, could not open the lid of the old linen chest, the wood had become so warped by extremes of cold and heat. All the same, there was a charm in this decay. The roses had reverted to a wild, primitive state, but it was a sturdy growth that bound the rickety stones together; just now the bushes were covered with almost cream buds that would open into wide, bee-coloured centres, and drop immediately afterwards as if drowned in their own scent. Yet it was only twenty years since the man had died, and barely ten since his son had moved to Noviodunum. It was lucky, Valerius thought, sitting down on his favourite seat; if the fellow had not been terrified of the Alemanni making a sudden raid, he would never have sold the place so cheaply. Otherwise, with the rising taxes and a centurion's pay always being in arrears, they would have had to live above the guardhouse down the road, and thus missed half the hunting.

Even Julia paused to glance at the tall grasses before she put some food and a little wine in front of her brother. He might dislike her going into the kitchen, she thought with some amusement, but at what other house in the region would he get such a loaf of bread? She had been thinking about this moment all the week, but Valerius liked to take his time; there was nobody so stubborn as he could be if he felt that she was trying to hurry him, and she was pondering what she could say that would neither provoke him nor turn his attention from the journey, when he startled her by beginning upon the subject himself.

"I saw Vinodius. The man's a fool."

Julia nodded. It was hardly wise to speak thus of the governor of a province, but her anxiety was too strong to rouse her to protest. "He made no difficulty about your pension, I hope?"

"Yes and no. It will come, but he begged me to remain in charge here till the autumn."

"Oh, Valerius! This is the second time."

"They are so short of men," Valerius answered uneasily, "with the troubles in Pannonia no reinforcements have arrived."

"But you were due to retire a year ago, and Vinodius persuaded you to stop for just one more season. You are always grumbling that unless you get your freedom soon, you will be too old for hunting parties. Besides, once you are no longer in command of the post, we can return, if you wish, to Ceresio."

"We are safe for another year. People talk against the eagles, but they will not rise against them. Still, I shall be thankful when new troops arrive. Half a legion would be sufficient."

"When we came here ten years ago, it was to guard the trading road to Lugdunum. Now we are an outpost."

Valerius shrugged his shoulders, and went on with his meal. He was glad to be home; the bread at Aventicum was poor, dry stuff, and they had charged him outrageous prices for a miserable drop of wine. He wondered how much he dared tell his sister? Brave as she was, all women were afraid of raiders. The Alemanni beyond the Rhine were on the move, although that did not necessarily mean that this province was in danger. There were excellent forts, both at Augusta Raurica and Vindonissa. Only the Helvetians themselves were discontented: not the farmers in the plains, but their much wilder cousins in the mountain valleys; and there was a chance, though he considered it to be a remote one, of a sudden attack upon an isolated Roman post. Strange as it seemed, and he looked at the hay wagon lumbering down the road with old Mocco trudging beside it in his flapping summer hat, they were now, as his sister had said, almost at the frontier. He noticed that Julia was staring at him, and said inconsequentially, "I often wonder why you have never married again."

"Don't tell me, Valerius, that you have entangled yourself with some praetor's daughter at Aventicum! I always told you that a slave girl is much less dangerous."

How like a sister, Valerius reflected, to reduce his remark to such a level! Naturally if a man was forced to remain in the depths of the country for most of the year, he needed a little pleasure when he got to the city. "No, Julia," he said, shaking his head firmly, "this journey I had no time for girls. But why should you work in the kitchen like a freedwoman? Marcus is rich, he would make you a good husband."

"Marcus is honest, it is a rare quality in these times; but I have no wish to marry him."

"Why not?" Valerius turned his glass so that it caught the light. There were only three goblets left unbroken, and Julia kept them solely for his use, refusing to drink herself from anything but the native pottery. It could not be loyalty to the memory of Gaius, he thought: he had always resented his father's choice of that dull and almost landless provincial for the beautiful girl that Julia had been; but the marriage had not lasted long, his brother-in-law had died from a fever two years afterwards in a campaign against the Dacians.

"Why not?" Julia echoed his question; then she looked across at the opposite woods and answered quietly, "I enjoy my liberty; and remember, Valerius, I am getting old."

"Old! You are seven years younger than I am!" Even in full sunlight it was astonishing how youthful Julia looked; she had the calm brow and the smooth cheeks of some statue of Juno. "I suppose it's the air; it's healthy here, and there are no distractions, but you look better than when you came. Don't say No to Marcus this summer. I saw one of his officers at Aventicum. Marcus is coming to visit us, after he makes his report next month."

"And Pennilocus is safe. Is it as bad as that?"

"Of course not," Valerius answered sharply. He was annoyed that his sister had again read the thoughts that he was trying to keep out of his own consciousness. "I want you to be happy. We have no friends here, and some winter night the roof is going to blow away. Come now, you have not answered my question," he continued, because Julia's grasp of his real motive had annoyed him, "why won't you marry Marcus?"

"I suppose I have my roots here." Night after night she wakened at the slightest noise, thinking that a rolling pebble was some barbarian's foot, or that the dog scratching itself was the slither of skins as the raiders slid over the wall; yet equally at dusk, as she wandered along the itinerant stream that divided Mocco's oats from her own orchard, she also wondered how she could leave the bushes that she had tended until they had become part of her, even if she could bear to accompany her brother when he returned to the vineyard at Ceresio that was all that was now left to them from their father's estate.

"If it's Veria, Marcus would let you keep her; besides, she must be almost of marriageable age herself."

"Veria! No, not Veria!" It was Julia's turn this time to be uneasy, because Valerius had blundered closer to the truth than she desired. "Still, I couldn't take the child to a fortress; like myself, she is used to liberty."

"But she isn't Roman."

"Sometimes, Valerius, on a day like this, when I see the water splashing out of the fountain, and the rock pinks opening up and down the banks, I think I have become Helvetian myself. It is cool here, even at midsummer. Do you remember at Ceresio, how the heat seemed to lie on us when we were children, as if we were drowning in it?"

"Marry Veria to someone, or take her with you. I suppose that the child is pretty, though I see very little of her, and you will have taught her to be diligent, but it is time that you return to civilization. It is your brother speaking." His attempt at seriousness only made Julia laugh.

"The days have gone when a man could be the tyrant of his family. Tell me, is her name Claudia . . . or Primula? I warn you, brother, it is going to be very difficult to get me out of the house."

Valerius almost snapped off the stem of his goblet with irritation. He poured out more wine than he had intended, and instead of mixing it with water, gulped most of it down before speaking again. "I was too busy talking to Vinodius, I told you, to have time for girls; besides," he added glumly, "the Treasury only opened on my last morning."

"So they paid you after all?" That was the information for which Julia had been waiting. Perhaps there would be enough to buy a third spinning wheel, and to have the roof repaired. Unless, of course, Valerius had made some foolish purchase, like the time when he had returned with a special breed of shepherd dog. The colour had washed out of the animal's coat in the first rains, and it had been an ordinary brute, similar to those bred in any of the neighbouring villages.

"Up to this spring. They even gave me the arrears." Valerius paused triumphantly to watch the effect of this declaration. "I got a new pair of hunting boots; I needed

19

them." He was afraid that Julia was going to rebuke him for extravagance, but she nodded gravely.

"Yes, our shoemaker here uses such rough leather and with your skin. . . ." Her brother had changed as well, she thought; the turbulence had gone, and much of the mockery. "They are not as good with their tools as our Ceresio people, but they farm better."

"I brought most of the money back with me. If I have to wait as long for my pension as I waited for my pay, we shall be in our graves before the roof is mended. Besides, everything was such a price; some idiotic rumour seems to have spread among the craftsmen, and a lot of them have moved to Lousonna. If the Emperor has a victory this summer, it will frighten the barbarians, and we shall get a better bargain in the autumn for whatever we decide to buy."

Julia nodded. It was unlike her brother to be so prudent, and confirmed her fears that the situation was worse than he would admit. They sat still on the terrace; neither of them wanted to move. It was almost noon, and the haymakers had stopped for a brief rest. The nearest peak on the distant horizon was almost free from snow. "You have never changed, Julia," Valerius said at last, "I remember when father took us to the temple of Apollo. You could not have been more than fourteen, but you said then that you would never marry. You wanted to hide, like Juno, in a hut among the chestnut woods."

"I have often thought that I was foolish not to have

remained there." It had been almost a vow, Julia thought, and she had never known such peace again. On that day she had been innocent and really young; she had wisdom now, but though it was deeper, it was also a broken thing; there were cares, she knew how people suffered.

"Julia! You would have died from the cold that first winter!"

Trained by the many years that they had been together, Julia did not answer, and Valerius, who had expected an indignant, "Not while I was under the protection of Apollo," finished his wine in silence. How much isolation there was between even those human beings who were near to one another; his sister seemed to have accepted widowhood and poverty and exile with a stoical gentleness, but she did not understand her brother. To her, Valerius reflected, he was all rebel and sinner. He wondered if she were even fond of her ward, Veria, the daughter of a freedwoman and an Helvetian soldier, and for whom, apparently, she was sacrificing her chance of a second marriage? No, it was not love for the child, he decided, looking at Julia's calm expression, it was simply her sense of duty.

"That was the happiest summer that we ever spent," Julia said, turning a little as if she did not want him to see her face. "Do you remember the afternoon that we went to swim near the Villa Poiana, and how the officials passed us in the state barge?"

"Yes," Valerius answered; his heart began to beat as if he had run up to the peak above the saddleback. "You mean the day that I saw Fabula, the day I dived for the white rose?"

The steps were really dangerous. Yet no man could be spared to mend them until the haymaking were over, and then what could they do but patch the surface? The stones were loose, and piled against a wall that was itself overgrown with tufts of grass and the thick leaves of a viscous, creeping sedum. Its roots and the frost had split the slabs, which rocked when Valerius trod on them, and the edges were crumbling into a fine, powdery dust. He kicked aside a pebble that was lying perilously under an ivy trail on the final block, and stepped down to the path that led to Rances.

Valerius paused, out of sheer habit, to look towards the guardhouse, but it was useless to descend to it in mid-afternoon. The men were in the fields; they were ditchers and road menders, there was little left of their military calling but the name. It displeased him, because he knew that they ought to be patrolling the hills and watching the border paths, but what could he do? One thing led to another. The peasants were frightened of the Alemanni, and moved, whenever they could, to the better protected villages in the south; then if the soldiers did not help to sow and plough, there was not enough food, and finally the road had to be kept in repair, or stores and reinforcements could not reach them. If only

Vinodius would not constantly withdraw men for the garrison at Aventicum! The fellows were far more useful here than mewed up behind walls.

The earth was silvery and thin on the steep bank at his left hand; sometimes a root emerged from the tangle of grass above it, to creep uncovered down the slope until it found another cleft where it could dig itself in, rather like Julia's words, he thought, as he paused for breath at the fork of the path. One way led to the village, and the other, upon which he now stood, to the milking huts above him on the hills. Julia's phrases were austere, precise; you listened to them unsuspiciously because they seemed parched and safe. What had she meant, flinging that name at him vengefully, a veritable Neptune's trident, so that all the nerves that he had supposed were dried away, or dead, had sprung at the sound into an ocean of revolt? It was not the height that made it hard to breathe; it was youth, his glory and disgrace, that swept and ebbed through his blood. He was dizzy with it, almost mad; and yet, suppose that fourteen years ago that incident at Poiana had never happened, what would he have known of happiness as a fat tribune in some sleepy city near Rome?

The rough track was hardly a path, it was a series of stepping stones of shorter grass leading from one bush to another. After an hour he would emerge into the light again, into thinner air and among those wild shrubs with red, curving blossoms and almost gritty leaves, that were both the signal and the banner of the Alps. There was no time today to go so high, all he wanted was to sit somewhere and think; so at the first clearing he found a favourite log, settled himself upon it as comfortably as possible, and opened his tunic.

Valerius scratched a rough map in the dust with the toe of his sandal. They were safe, he supposed, for a year; for five, if reinforcements came. Eventually, through sheer weight of numbers, the barbarians would cross the Rhine. He could almost smell the roof burning, and feel the glass and enamel crushing under his feet. He had seen a sacked camp and plenty of looted villages during his service in Pannonia, that land of hidden ambushes in silent snow, where the wind was often more of a killer than the armies. He never wanted to hear a war cry nor the clang of the alarm again. He had expected to die in that campaign, and he still did not know if his recall, not to Italy but to Aventicum, was due to chance or to some final intervention by his father. The narrowness of provincial life had been insupportable after his battle experience, and he had soon volunteered for service at Orba. It had cost him a promotion but he had gained his liberty, even if it had turned him from a soldier into a farmer.

The frontier had been quiet upon his arrival. He had received his pay regularly, and had hunted a good deal. It had not seemed worth while spending much upon the house, because after his discharge, he had intended to return to Ceresio. Then his parents had died, Julia had joined him, the Villa Orba had grown round them

24

both; gradually he had come to feel that the fields about him were his own. That dream had broken when the Alemanni had infiltrated the hills during the previous year. Led by runaway slaves, they had shot a herdsman or two, carried off some cattle, and disappeared before the alarm could be given, but the day was coming when they would thunder across the plain as naturally and wastefully as the avalanche that had smothered two fields of the best corn, a summer ago, east of Rances.

It was pleasantly cool, and the light, falling through the leaves, made gay patterns the width of the log. There was a world in miniature on the stone at his feet; tiny silver trees of moss crept up the cracks from a swamp of green spores and a headland of pebbles. Perhaps he had drunk too much wine in the city, or on the terrace to spite Julia, he felt so drowsy. After his discharge, if there was still time left, he must come up here to dream, to think about the universe, about that place beyond the mysteries where, some philosophers said, neither winds nor combat existed. Pictures began to form in his head as he closed his eyes, he felt his head drop forward. . . . "Have you nothing better to do than sleep on a day like this?" an indignant voice demanded.

Those or words like them had been Fabula's first greeting; memories spun dizzily back to him. He started expectantly, but it was only old Grumbler coming up to lick his hands, and the creature looking at him was not Fabula; it was neither boy nor girl but a bit of moving landscape, with a tunic looped up above dirty knees and burrs clinging to its uncombed hair.

"You can't have been hunting, Veria," he said stupidly, "it's not the season."

"Of course not. Domina Julia sent me up with the goats; she would not let me go haymaking."

"Who is with them now?" he asked indifferently. He disliked girls from his household running wild as goatherds, but as he could not afford to have another servant, it was difficult to protest. There was so little Roman left in the child anyhow, that he understood why his sister hesitated to take her to Pennilocus.

"Nennius. Domina Julia sent him up to me an hour ago, and I can tell you I was glad to see him."

"Yes, goats are stupid animals. It must be lonely sitting for hours among those rocks."

"Oh, it's not that! I like watching them; each has got a different nature, and they will eat one plant and leave another, for no reason that I can discover. It wasn't the goats, it was this. . . ." Veria held out something on the palm of what was less a hand than a paw.

"The Alemanni!" Valerius sprang to his feet. "It's one of their arrowheads. Where did you find it?"

"Close to the milking hut. It hasn't been there long, but it's had the dew on it," Veria said professionally. "Nennius and I think that the archer lost it yesterday. Grumbler got down a slope, and couldn't get up again. She's beginning to grow very old. I scrambled along to

26

her and found it, lying below a rock. It's heavier than our hunting arrows, and the shape is different."

"The man may still be there."

"At first I was almost frightened," Veria lied. Actually she had been so terrified that she had stopped on her hands and knees, feeling eyes on her everywhere, and hardly able to breathe. It was a common practice to trap herdsmen and sell them as slaves beyond the Rhine. "I thought the shooter might be watching me, but it was open ground, there were no dislodged stones nor signs of footsteps, so I took the arrow, and climbed back to the hut as quickly as I could. I met Nennius coming up the path, and he found the shaft. It had broken off near the head, and was lying, a few paces away, down the ravine. He thinks the man was hungry and wanted to shoot a goat, but when he missed, he was afraid to crawl out and recover the arrow, for fear he would be seen. Nennius is behind me, bringing down the goats; he sent me on to give the alarm."

"They would choose the moment when we are all cutting hay," Valerius grumbled. For the first time he looked at the child with some interest; she was calm but she had understood the danger. "Come along; the sooner the guard is out the better, and I must send a couple of fellows up to help Nennius. But Veria," she looked up in surprise because it was the first time that he had addressed her as an equal, and not as a child, "it will be better not to speak about the arrow to Domina Julia. We need not alarm her. I shall tell her simply that strangers have been noticed in the hills." Their eyes met in a look of mingled duplicity and understanding; then both turned to race, as quickly as the rough grass allowed, along the zigzag pathway towards Orba.

There was a crackle in the air. Valerius started up for the tenth time since he had come to his couch. It must be some insect, because the watchdogs were silent. He was proud of his capacity to fall asleep at once, and this wakefulness annoyed him. It was absurd to let the chance discovery of an arrowhead destroy his inner tranquillity; some goatherd could have bartered cheese for it in the local market, and then lost it in the hills; Vinodius—and whatever you might think of the man's incompetence, he was still the governor of the province —Vinodius had assured him that the frontier was peaceful. It had been necessary to take precautions, but if the Alemanni were really in the hills in force, they were within striking distance of Aventicum, and that was unthinkable. No, he was a fool to be so wakeful; perhaps it was the city food, or the unseasonable weather, because after a long, wet spring, midsummer had come over night. He would sleep, he must sleep. . . . He turned and wondered if Julia had noticed anything, but she had seemed unusually gay at supper, and as for Veria, the way that she had laughed when the serving maid had dropped the butter, you would never suspect that she knew one weapon from the other. "Are you frightened?" he had asked, as they had come within sight of Orba, and she had panted, "Not of dying, only of being a slave." Perhaps there was more Roman in her than he had supposed? Her mother, the daughter of their head spinning woman at Ceresio, had been brought up with his sister, and had been, so they had joked, Julia's shadow. It had even been arranged that she should marry a young soldier who had come, oddly enough, from the district round Minnodunum, on the day of Julia's own wedding. How little any of them had imagined that they would ever see the man's country! He had been killed in the Dacian campaign, Veria's mother had died, and when Julia had come to Orba, she had brought the orphan with her.

Valerius turned over again, stretched out his legs, and flung back the covers. He was too restless; perhaps if he sat outside for a while, drowsiness would come to him. He got up, slipped on an old tunic, and went through his private door into the garden.

It was dark and almost cold as he stepped on to the terrace. The many sounds that composed the summer night were audible as he paused, and to distract himself he divided their unity; that was water sliding over distant stones, the rustle was Grumbler turning round in her straw, the drip of the fountain, the slither of mouse or lizard inside the broken walls, added to, rather than lessened, the impression of solitude. Then he let the noises flow together again in a whole, and matched them to the times. How long would Gallien be able to hold the Guards before they rebelled again and elected a new Emperor in his place? The farmers, he supposed, would continue to hide their grain from a Treasury that taxed them but could offer no security in return. Why did Vinodius trust the word of the tribes beyond the Rhine? The Alemanni had the instincts of gladiators and the appetites of wolves. If half the tribute money (for this was what those gifts to the chiefs really were) had been spent upon paying and feeding good soldiers, there would still be an empire's peace along the imperial roads. If . . . then Valerius paused, it was chilly, yet he was too lazy to fetch his cloak, if . . . at this moment the watchdogs started up, snarling and tugging at their chains; he could hear nailed sandals thumping along the gravel, and he saw a torch, about fifty yards from the gate. "Quiet," he shouted, for he recognized the voice of Quintus, the under-officer whom he had sent up to the milking hut, "quiet, dogs, they are friends."

By this time all the inhabitants of the villa were awake. Boys ran out with more torches, the dogs were in a frenzy, a baby began to wail, everybody was shouting at each other. Valerius hurried through the house and down towards the main gate. He reached it just as the first soldiers arrived.

"Quintus!" he shouted. "What has happened?"

"We come in peace." Quintus mimicked the traders' greeting, and although it was too dark to see his face, it was evident by the tone of his voice that he was very much amused. Then Nennius came forward with a torch, and Valerius saw beyond his own soldiers a gesticulating group of strangers and the dark outline of two mules.

"I set two guards," Quintus explained, "and the rest of us went to sleep in the hut. A man woke me, there was shouting along the crest of the hill. I drew up the men in battle order, and Nennius crawled forward to see what was happening. He came back with six captives, taken singlehanded! It was a Greek trader and his men. The Alemanni surprised them in the pass above Saltus. Two of them are wounded, but not badly."

"Aie! Aie! I am hurt to death," a bundle groaned from the back of a mule.

"It's mostly fright, he has a flesh wound in the arm," Quintus observed without pity.

"Aie! My arm! My arm! The Alemanni were as thick as wolves about me, only the darkness saved us."

"They were a bowshot or more away from you," Quintus retorted.

"And what were you doing in the mountains?" Valerius asked gruffly. "What is your name?"

"Demetrius. Demetrius of Corinth, now of Verona. I have just come from the garrison at Vindonissa. You can ask the governor about me. He will tell you that I am an honest man, and that I can get you anything you want, from Rhaetian wine to glass or the best hunting dogs."

Valerius lifted a torch from the boy at his side and looked at the trader. He was a short man, crouched on the mule, hugging his wounded arm and moaning.

"Aie! Have pity on me! I swear to you, it was the governor's own servant who told us of the pass at Saltus. If it had not been for the gods, I should never have seen Verona again. Hear me, I shall sacrifice a kid to Hermes directly I get home."

"The governor's servant," Valerius snorted. "You were creeping round the backway, to avoid paying tolls."

"I *swear* no such thought ever entered my head. The man at Vindonissa assured me it was safe. Now I am wounded, and have lost two sacks of meal, paid for with hard-earned silver the day before yesterday."

"One," Quintus corrected. "They threw one sack away as bait to the raiders, but we stacked the other in the hut so as to put the wounded on the mules."

"The arrow has rent my cloak. I am only a poor, unprotected trader . . ."

"Be silent!" Valerius commanded. "Perhaps this will teach you to keep to the highway in future. As you are hurt, you have my permission to stay here for the night, but tomorrow we will have a little conversation about tolls. Take them to the guest room, and send a woman with the wound salve," he continued, looking round the semicircle of faces, "but remember, I do not wish Domina Julia to be disturbed."

A boy yelped as a bit of hot resin from a torch rolled

32

on to his fingers. The dogs started growling again as the gate was opened and the mules were led into the courtyard. He saw Veria, in a dirty and ragged hunting tunic, chattering eagerly to Nennius. Figures moved away slowly, some towards the stables, others into the house. It resembled the end of one of those long religious processions of his boyhood, when the road had slowly cleared as the tired worshippers returned to their homes, and he alone had waited for the last flames to flicker down, with an indefinable sense of disappointment that the stars were as cold as ever above him, and that there was no answer, from nature or man, to either doubt or hope.

"They all tell the same story," Quintus said, rubbing a fleck of earth from his belt with his thumb. "Some fool at Vindonissa told them about this pass and then, just as they had crossed the summit, the arrows hit them without warning. It can't have been a regular ambush, or none of them would have got away alive."

"Did they see their attackers?"

"They say no, except the guide. He says he saw two men running, more than a bowshot away."

"But it could have been thieves?"

"I doubt it." Quintus shook his head. "They would have closed in and slaughtered the party. They were carrying a lot of bales."

"Yet they told me at Aventicum that the frontier was particularly quiet."

Quintus did not reply. What did that drunken, chaplet-wearing crowd know about boundaries, or outpost duty on a winter night, when the wind smote through two layers of sheepskin, and snow melted into the top of a man's boots? Once or twice he had thought that it would be pleasant to lie in the baths and have a slave bring ointments to him, but the smell of the salve had made him feel sick, and he much preferred the heavy local grapes to that thin, dark wine that the officers imported from Italy. He would much rather trust the drovers from Vindonissa if he wanted some news. This year, next year, something was going to happen, and when it did, those pseudo-commanders would scramble back into the next safe garrison and give veterans like himself a chance. Yes, he still might become a centurion before he died. "Three of the men need cloaks," he said, looking at Valerius with devotion. Valerius had given him his first step up the ladder, an appointment as under-officer the previous year.

"You should have heard that fellow at the Treasury when I asked for replacements! Still, I can't help wondering myself what they do with all the grain they get. We had a good harvest last season. And if we had another fifty men, the frontier would take care of itself." The words were a commonplace of the border, but as he said them, Valerius realized their falsity for the first time. It was too late for fifty men, too late for a legion.

They were facing a gigantic movement that they could no more hold than they could hold a flood. "It's strange," he continued, "just as the world begins to learn something about civilization, some nation or some catastrophe comes along and destroys the knowledge."

Quintus looked up in surprise. "I am a simple man," he grunted, "and no philosopher. To me it is only a matter of spears, boots, and a good heart. The Alemanni are no better fighters than we are."

"They are not so good, but there are more of them. Tell me, Quintus, do you really think that those men were the advance guard of a raiding party?"

Quintus shook his head again; he was thinking regretfully of his last evening with the drovers. "Round Vindonissa they think it will come next year. It's not a city like Aventicum; they are frontier people, you can trust them."

"Then who do you think the men were? The trader was wounded, and there was that arrowhead. Do not be afraid to speak, I value your opinion," Valerius added encouragingly. Quintus was voluble enough in a wine shop, but did not always find it easy to talk to a superior officer.

"I think that they were two or three men sent out by the Alemanni to look at the land. Not thieves, because the village people took some cows up to those very slopes last week, and not a beast is missing. They probably wanted to shoot a goat, to provide food for their return journey. Nor did they want to be seen, or they would have killed the trader. They may have only seen his mule at first, and when they missed it, they ran, in case the party gave the alarm."

"If that is so, the attack may come this summer."

"I doubt it; they are good soldiers, and it is a part of their training. They want to know exactly where our positions are."

"I hope it will not start a panic in the village."

"Oh, no," Quintus answered indifferently; he was still thinking about the cloaks, and whether he dare ask for a new tunic for himself. "They'll talk. They always do. But nothing will happen."

It was strange, Valerius reflected, the Helvetians apparently accepted this state between war and peace almost as if it were natural. He had heard a man shout to his brother in the field, "Leave the roots of that stump alone; *they'll* be here next summer, why do their work for them?" Yet most of them did not migrate, nor did they attempt to build defences; was it passive resignation, or some incurable hope that the armies would spare their village? He glanced up, and saw that another strip had peeled from the painted wall during his absence. Half the chariot of the Sun was still there; but now the wheels had gone, and the hind legs of both the horses. He prided himself upon his lack of superstition, but tonight this seemed an omen, even to himself. Besides, he was tired and wanted to be alone. "Do the best you can for the equipment with this," he said wearily, handing a heavy silver coin to Quintus, who was watch-

36

ing him with greedy eyes. "It comes from my own pay, and is all that I can spare you."

"Sit here," Julia said, "and you will be in the shade." She helped Demetrius to cross to the stone seat, under some vines that had been trained over palings. There were still patches of long grass left in the valley, but most of the haymaking had ended, and a couple of long, low wagons were moving slowly towards the barn. "Try to rest," she added, "and I will bring you some leek juice presently. There is nothing so good as leeks after a fever."

How like his sister, Valerius moaned to himself; not only had she insisted upon looking after that wretched object on the bench, but now she had brought the fellow out at the precise moment when he, Valerius, was about to take his midday rest! It had always been an unwritten law that this part of the terrace was reserved for Julia and himself.

"Better?" he grunted, getting up and walking over to Demetrius. The man's face was neither coffee-coloured nor its natural brown, but an unhealthy, pallid, yes, you had to call it that, green.

"Aie! The pain! This is a terrible year."

"Why, if one of my soldiers had a scratch like yours, he would have reported back to duty the following day."

The eyes blinked at him. Valerius expected an out-burst of protestations; he knew what traders were like, all cunning and untruthfulness. Instead, the man answered with a disarming simplicity, "But sir, I am no longer young."

Nor am I, Valerius thought. He considered the unwelcome visitor for a moment; perhaps he had been unjust. He did not actually know how bad the wound might be; after he had forbidden Julia to attend to the man's arm, she had simply risen from her seat and had hardly spoken to him since. "Has my sister been looking after you well?" he enquired.

"I am very grateful to Domina Julia," the man said. Unexpectedly, Valerius fancied that he winked. "She has given me more herbs to drink than I knew came out of the earth."

"And no wine?"

"No, she says it is bad for a wound."

"Women are like that. Always afraid of things. I prefer them on a couch."

"You would like a slave girl?" Demetrius jerked forward so suddenly that he jarred his arm, and groaned.

"Not in these times."

"I could get you a pretty child at Vindonissa, and have her sent to you under guard. Along the highway, of course."

"For five hundred sesterces, no doubt."

"Aie! Prices are high this year; but with all these thieves about, they are likely to increase. The barbarians capture the girls before they reach our markets. But after all your hospitality I would not count the cost of the journey, nor," he added reluctantly, "the guard."

Valerius saw the trader measuring with his eye the patches on the broken wall, and was irritated that their poverty was uncovered.

"When I want a girl, I will find one for myself," he said curtly.

Demetrius nodded indifferently. "Perhaps you are right; this is hardly a good moment. But would you like a hunting dog? I have just one left, a beautiful animal; the governor of Vindonissa bought its brother."

"If you mean that flea-bitten object that I ordered them to shut up in the tool shed so that it did not contaminate my own pack, a thousand times no!" Veria was nursing the beast, he knew; he had seen her take a saucer of milk to the creature only that morning. Once the child grew up, she would be just as austere as his sister.

"It *is* pure Molossian, but the journey was hard on us all."

"Keep to the highway, pay your tolls, and you will be safe."

Demetrius shrugged his good shoulder. "How is a poor man to live? I tramp these dusty roads, and then catch fever in the rains. I wait for hours at some official's door, and it may be nightfall before a slave tells me that his master is invited to a banquet and has no time for my wares. Before I can even set foot within my own

39

city, the tax collector takes half of what I have earned, and anything that he fancies from my baggage. And where has he been during the summer? Never a foot further than the forum or the baths!"

It seemed a pity, Valerius thought, that the coloured border round the villa would have to be cut the following day. The ground spread below them like a mosaic pavement, full of thousands of flowers whose names he did not know, instead of stones. There were yellow claws spotted with black, pale-blue heads that seemed to open every year at the exact moment when the sickles were sharpened, occasional poppies, or a clump of tall grass. It was hot; he wanted to sprawl on the bench where the merchant was sitting in his favourite corner, and he yawned.

"What markets we could have!" Demetrius swept his unhurt arm the length of the horizon, as if he could see a dozen new settlements between them and Lousonna; then he noticed Valerius staring at him suspiciously, and laughed. "No, I am not a spy. I have had nothing to do with the tribes, though I could name you plenty who have, and many of them Roman. I was only thinking of the hundreds who still cannot tell a goblet from a cooking pot, and of how much we could sell to them once they had settled."

"Sell! They would slit your throat."

"Oh, not necessarily mine; I am not a Roman officer. No, there is a lot of trade going on now at Vindonissa, but it means changing to different wares, and alas, this year," he looked up very seriously, "I had nothing in my packs that was suitable."

There was something so disarming in the trader's frankness that in spite of himself Valerius joined in the laughter. "How does this barter go on," he enquired, "are the chiefs allowed into the city?"

"No, not the chiefs. They send messengers, usually among the drovers. Cattle are cattle, and the men who are able to handle them on roads are rare. They form a band among themselves, and an outsider has no chance with them." Demetrius scratched an ear mournfully. "I once exchanged a jar of the best olive oil for a cow, without taking one of them to help me, and the wretched beast died on my hands the next morning."

"And does the commander of the garrison know about these . . . guests?"

"Of course. He buys from them himself. Oh, nothing much, some pelts for a cloak, or a bowl of winter honey. Most of the firewood that they burn during the winter comes from the Alemanni along the frontier. The best forests are their side of the Rhine. You can get good bargains sometimes, really fine skins in exchange for our carved brooches, or some of our big corals. They would give half they have for weapons, but the sale of these is forbidden. It's ten lashes if you as much as show them a dagger."

Valerius nodded. It sounded exactly like Pannonia. "What are the Alemanni like?" he asked. "I have only spoken to captives."

"The usual barbarians. Strong, healthy, stupid. Too dangerous to make good slaves. When they have nothing else to do, they kill each other. It would be easy to deal with them, apart from two things."

"And these are . . . ?" Valerius waited expectantly.

"Their numbers—there are a thousand of them to every hundred of your legionaries—and their love of fighting. It's life to them, and an unwelcome duty to you."

"There's little enough to eat," Valerius grumbled, "without destroying more crops." Yet the trader's words were true. He looked down at the straight road leading towards Aventicum, and knew that he grudged taking his soldiers out of the fields to keep an almost idle watch along the hills. There was so much to do, and never enough men to finish the tasks properly. How happily he could live as a farmer when his service was over, if the frontier were quiet, if . . . but here his conscience began to mock him. He could dedicate his sword in the temple, but he could not leave the memories that were his far-away youth suspended upon a wall. It was their harshness and their fragrance that he remembered in his sleepless hours, and not whether the spotted cow had had, or had not had, its calf.

"Yes, they would be comparatively easy to destroy, because they quarrel easily among themselves and split into scattered groups. Rome had unity," Demetrius wriggled round to find a more comfortable position for his arm; "now even the unity has gone."

It irritated Valerius to hear a wretched Greek merchant making such comments; but with one emperor in Rome and another in Gaul, he could not deny the statement, though he was not going to let such an observation pass unreproved. "People have grown selfish," he announced pompously, "each province thinks only of itself. Yet it is the administration that matters, and this continues, no matter who may be ruler. Still, I sometimes think that we have discovered too much; we have exchanged our virtues for spices. The world has become too big."

Demetrius stared across the valley with an expression of deep misery on his face. He could not sit still, and occasionally he moaned, he jerked, or he rocked backwards and forwards, as if the mere act of movement might relieve his aching arm.

"Where are you going from here?" Valerius asked.

"First to Aventicum, then to Lousonna." The black eyes looked up anxiously, as if these words were a summons to leave the villa. "My overseer is sick. The lady, your sister, said that neither of us would be able to ride a mule for another week."

"Yes, you had a servant who was hurt as well."

"Felix, my overseer, an invaluable fellow though he is a Christian; the wound was nothing, but he has a fever," the trader pleaded. "We are trespassing upon your hospitality too long, but perhaps there is a room in the village . . . though there is no inn there."

Valerius did not reply, he hated people who fawned; instead, he snapped off a withered tendril, and tossed it into the field before he said sharply, "I was at Aventicum a week ago. The road is in good repair."

"The commander at Vindonissa gave me a recommendation to the governor. I have a cloak that might suit him, lined with beautiful furs."

"Bought from the Alemanni, no doubt."

"I got it from an Helvetian hunter," Demetrius answered indignantly, "it cost me silver, and the best knife I had."

Yes, the sale of weapons was forbidden, Valerius thought grimly, but there was nothing to prevent that hunter from slipping across the border and selling his knife on the next dark night. He said nothing, however, because the women were starting down the path to the field, the siesta was over, and the wretched fellow in front of him had deprived him of his sleep. Yet he dared not annoy Julia again; he hated to enter the house when she was in one of what he called her "injured" moods.

"You must arrange with my sister," he said, rising and stretching himself, "she will tell you where she wishes you to stay. I must get back to my vines." Demetrius bowed with the guilty air of a slave who had just escaped a beating, and babbled, "May your charity be rewarded." Then bowing again, and clutching his arm, he added, and the impudence of it kept Valerius in a rage during the whole of his walk down the hill, "I would exchange my Molossian hound for half a sack of meal. The animal is pure bred and well schooled, it only needs rest."

44

II

━━━━━━━━━━━━━━━━

VALERIUS stretched himself and yawned; he had
just awakened from a sound sleep. It was the first
time for over a week that he had had the bench to
himself, and in the interval the nodules on the vines
above him had turned into tiny grapes. Demetrius had
left that morning, after many protestations of gratitude,
and with a third mule that he had contrived to purchase
cheaply from a neighbouring farmer. Now the place
was his own again at last. Valerius stared at the meadows, where the grass was beginning to grow after the
first hay, and at the neighbouring field of barley. Before
they could count the days, the grain would be ripe.

"Valerius!" He looked up at his sister in surprise.
This was the second time that she had broken the rule
that his noon rest was never to be disturbed. "Yes,
Julia," he answered, "has something happened?"

"I wondered if you would have time to look at that
tree that is blocking up the stream." Julia had her
arms full of linen; she was taking it to dry along the
top of the orchard.

"The tree? Yes, I had forgotten it." An old trunk covered with lichen had toppled into the water earlier in the year. "I shall bathe in the river afterwards; can you ever remember so hot a summer?"

"Oh, Valerius," Julia twisted a towel into a knot between her fingers, "I am so anxious about Veria. Only yesterday, she asked me for a new tunic."

Valerius shrugged his shoulders. His sister had decided that the girl had fallen in love with Nennius. She had even persuaded the trader to take the boy with him for a short time to Aventicum. "I am sure that you are mistaken," he said, "they are both children."

"Then why are they always running off into the mountains together? Besides, she goes about as if she were in a dream."

"Demetrius would have given you an amber brooch. You saved his servant's life." Felix, a surly fellow who was said to be a Christian, had almost died, not from the arrow scratch but from a fever.

"What should I do with an amber brooch?" Julia asked bitterly.

"You could wear it when Marcus comes to visit us," her brother said. Then, seeing the irritation in her face, he added, "Suppose they are in love with each other, would it matter? The boy will be old enough to join the legion next year, and his father was an excellent soldier."

"Valerius!" Julia looked up, wondering why her brother was so stupid. "The boy was born here, and both his parents were Helvetian. Veria is a Roman citizen. I have always considered her my ward, and one of our family."

"She has no dowry, and I often wonder how much longer I can afford to remain a citizen myself. If I had not had my pay last month, I might have had to pawn my armour."

"The child is not old enough to marry." Julia flung the towels over the wall instead of taking them to the orchard, as if she were numbed by some fatigue of the soul.

"I will go and look at the tree," Valerius said. In such a mood no explanations would satisfy his sister, and he did not want to quarrel with her. "If Mocco comes to ask about the wagon shaft, tell him to return and see me after supper."

The path followed the course of the stream. Valerius had seen its beginnings high up in the mountains, where the water smashed over tiny, polished boulders, or raced between two lips of Alpine grass. It was tranquil here, almost sluggish; it would increase its speed only where it joined the river, and after that, he thought philosophically, it would be the same as other currents, no longer individual water, but as lost as a friend marching in the tortoise formation, with his shield over his head.

There was the tree. Its roots were in the air, and there was a branch on the upper side that still had some green leaves on it. A familiar figure got up from the bank as he approached. "Domina Julia said that you would be coming here," Veria said, "so I brought an extra towel; it would be a pity not to bathe on a day like this."

He looked at the girl intently, but could see no trace of unhappiness on that sunburnt face. "Has she been talking to you?" Veria asked. "I'm not in love with Nennius, though she thinks I am. I only said that it was unfair to send him to Aventicum. I should like to see the temples and the statues as well, and I am tired of being told to bring this or fetch that from morning till night. Domina Julia has scolded me all the year."

This was true. Valerius knew that he ought to take his sister's part; but ever since the incident on the hillside there had been a bond between Veria and himself. He had even tried to shield her from his sister's tongue.

"It is some passing melancholy," he suggested, "Julia is often angry with me as well."

"She has been unhappy ever since she quarrelled with the tribune last summer."

"Quarrelled? With Marcus?"

"I thought you knew." Veria leaned over with the supreme confidence of the young, and flicked his arm with a rush. It had the silky feeling of a tassel. "He left suddenly, yes. We had planned to make a hunting trip when he had a message from Pennilocus. I never knew that his departure had anything to do with my sister." It had been a relief at the time, Valerius remembered; Marcus was too energetic; he had wanted to scramble about the hills all day as if he had been in training for a foot race. "He is dull," he continued, "but he is a good soldier."

"And believes in the family!" Veria's voice was so passionately indignant that Valerius smiled. "You seem to dislike him," he grunted.

Veria nodded gratefully. "He believes that a Roman girl should neither speak nor be seen abroad; why, he would have stopped my hunting had he known about it, but I used to creep away as soon as it was light, while he was lingering in the courtyard waiting for Domina Julia to come to the fountain."

"Then why did they quarrel?" It would be such a suitable match, and when he retired it would be pleasant to have the villa to himself.

"He flattered her, and they agreed in theory about the Roman virtues. According to his rules, she should have passed him with her eyes fixed on the ground, and a veil over her head; instead she picked grapes for him, when we were not allowed to touch them."

"And I thought it was the birds."

"Domina Julia pretends that she likes the country, but it is three springs since she climbed up to the milking huts; all she does now is to wash and scold. That's the reason that so many pieces are coming out of the floor. She throws sand on the pavement and scrubs, until even the bits of stone rebel and come loose. I know

49

she thinks it is sinful to be idle, but she sits by that old statue in the woods for hours."

"Come, Veria, you must not exaggerate. Julia clung to home even when she was a child. But you still haven't told me why they quarrelled."

"Family, of course. I was coming back through the woods one evening, with a bird that Nennius had shot, when I heard their voices. I dodged behind a tree, because I did not want to meet them, and I heard the tribune say, 'It happened so long ago that nobody remembers it.' I could not hear her reply, but he answered almost impatiently, 'It is really not as important as you imagine.' Then she cried, and I ran away before they found me; but the tribune left the next day."

"Long ago!" Valerius groaned. "She is still thinking of what she calls our disgrace. Oh women. . . ." He snapped a twig from the dead branch beside him, and flung it viciously into the water.

"Suppose you tell me about Fabula?"

"Fabula!" Valerius looked up in astonishment. For years the name had never crossed his lips; then after his conversation with Julia on the day that they had brought Demetrius to the villa, it had hummed through every thought like a swarm of new bees. "Where did you hear that word?" he asked.

"Domina Julia said that you had been sent to Pannonia because of her. But she would never tell me the real story. Sometimes the weavers talk." A lizard popped its head out between two stones, almost as if it were listening to them; then a pebble slipped, and, startled by the noise, it vanished again.

"I told you that I was not in love with Nennius," Veria pleaded.

"It is not a story for young girls."

"I have seen calves born, and helped Mocco's wife after she lost her baby."

It was true, Valerius thought, he was being guilty of the same fault as his sister; what was the use of applying the rules of an imperial court to this child who had grown up in the woods? She was used to the howling of wolves in winter; she had helped to herd the flocks almost since she could walk. Besides, ever since Julia's chance remark, a second spring was thundering through his blood; in spite of the disturbances on the frontier and the presence of Demetrius on his private terrace, he felt young again, and almost light-headed. "It was a golden summer," he began, "a season such as I have never known since; there was a cool, dry air under the intense heat, and we lived in the water. I was at home for my first leave after training, and expected to be posted to a company. You cannot remember Ceresio, but the chestnut woods come down to the lake, and there are edges of sand between the gardens.

"Julia always liked festivals, so when we heard that there was to be a procession by water from one of the inlets to the opposite temple, I took our little boat, and we sailed or rowed until I found a cove that seemed utterly deserted. Julia was anxious because we were underneath a garden wall that was covered with white roses, but, as I told her, the sand was free and we were doing the owners no harm. She cared for swimming as little as she cares now for hunting, but she sat there, resting, with her head on her hand and her eyes on the trees, until it was almost noon. Then the barges arrived, with great awnings that were almost purple, special hangings that had been lent to the boats for the day. There was one as dark blue as the lake itself, with a scroll pattern worked in gold along the border. The rowers had on short, white tunics, and the flutes and the oars rose and fell in an identical pattern. I could see Julia murmuring a prayer to Apollo, although I suspect that I was more akin to the priests, watching the scene as I did—for it overwhelmed me with the power of its beauty—than if I had sat there mumbling the habitual words. We watched the barges until they were almost out of sight, and then I glanced up at the stone above my head. It had a painted inscription on it that had been partly washed away by the rains. 'Why,' I said, and I remember how startled Julia looked, 'this must be the Tiger's villa.' The Tiger was my commander; we called him that because he was usually asleep, and then he would spring suddenly at some poor wretch who had no influence, and disgrace him in front of us all, for no valid reason. 'Then we must go at once,' Julia scolded, packing the food we had not eaten back into our basket; but I laughed and shook my head. 'Not till I've had my swim.' And then, the gesture was so unlike her, Julia picked a rose from the wall, and flung it into the water. 'Dive for that,' she said, 'then we'll go home.'

"The shingle sloped too much, so I scrambled on to a rock; but before I dived I looked across at the garden. There was a goddess coming down the path. No, Veria, don't smile, she was something beyond us mortals; there were no maids with her, and I could see the outline of her body under her transparent tunic, so I knew that she was going to bathe. We looked at each other, but she did not scream, and in my confusion I dived. I found the flower, and as I came up to the surface with the stem in my hand, I heard a voice mocking me, 'What a hunter! He dives for roses.'

" 'Only for bait,' I answered, bowing. 'I need a special lure when I hunt lynxes.'

"She did not give me the answer that I had expected, about not being nocturnal, or preferring fans to fur in July; she only motioned me to climb over the wall and sit beside her. 'I think I know your plumed helmet,' she teased; 'it nodded when you were my husband's escort, when was it, that sultry day we had the thunderstorm.' It was true that I had almost gone to sleep while the old fool was making some orations about his ancestors, but I had not known that anybody had seen me. Anyhow, before I could get over my confusion, I was standing, dripping wet, in front of her, in a hollow between two banks of willow. We talked for a few moments, and then I heard footsteps. 'I left my sister on

53

the beach,' I said, 'let me come back and see you tomorrow.'

" 'I never make promises,' she laughed, 'but this is a cool place to rest.' I must have glanced around to see if she had her women near her, because she added, 'I come here alone, to say my prayers.'

" 'Till tomorrow,' I whispered, because I knew that she must not meet Julia, and I sprang into the water again. My sister was half way up the shingle; she had heard our voices, but I pretended that I had merely spoken to a girl who was mending nets. I suspect now that she never believed my story, but she made no comment at the time. Remember," Valerius added anxiously, "I am not so much to blame as Julia says. The Tiger may have seen us, but he had no witnesses; he could not prove that I was inside his garden, and my father was selling land at the time, to pay for my equipment and for Julia's dowry."

"And you never heard what happened to her afterwards?"

"There was a divorce, but this was later, and then she disappeared."

"And was Fabula the only person whom you loved?" Veria asked, snapping off another reed.

"Of course not," Valerius chuckled, "there were dozens; only my sister did not know about them. Fabula had an intelligence of the body as well as the mind; that made her different from the others."

The silver green of the split grasses moved gently

in a tiny, welcome breeze. Veria flung her reeds into the stream, and watched them float towards the river. "Did you go back the following day?" she asked, moving over to sit beside him.

"Yes, and for several weeks afterwards. It was the hottest summer; every moment was more wonderful than its fellow. I contrived to get my leave extended; verily the gods blessed us. Julia was angry; I suppose I neglected her, but she kept her woes to herself. I rowed away to the garden every morning, and at noon, while the rest of Ceresio was asleep, Fabula joined me by the willows. We used to talk about immortality, but not in the sense that Julia understood the word; it had nothing to do with duty. No, it was a state, Fabula said, of seeing."

Perhaps it would not seem new to him now, Valerius thought, but during that July the boy whom he met by chance along the road was a messenger of the Muses, the dusty Roman Empire was to cast its skin, everything was to be young again. "She wanted to go to Delphi," Valerius continued. "Her devotion to Apollo was the only link she had with Julia. There was a temple opposite us, on the top of the mountain, but the doctrine is austere for a woman." He seemed to feel her breasts under his hands again, and the cool skin that had sharpened his own fever. "We did not talk philosophy all the time. We made love. . . ."

" 'In a cave of rushes and silver willows,' " Veria quoted from a song maliciously.

55

"Not in a cave, but we used the rushes to shelter us. I never noticed their colour."

How different Orba was from that zone that had seemed purely water. The meadows here were wide and open, bands of green mixed with feathery flowers, smelling of the soil they grew in, while the stream itself was as straight as a spear shaft. A few faded thistles, and a purple spike whose name he did not know, waved stiffly above the grass. "We talked, and made our offerings to Aphrodite," he said slowly, because it was a relief to talk about Fabula at last, "and she said that we were in some group apart; neither better nor worse than her husband and Julia, but different. The old tradition of Delphi had isolated us; we had come to be outside what she called Rome. I could not always follow what she meant, but I liked to watch the thoughts moving across her face as if they were birds flying away from winter. One day I was late; I had waited till some fishermen rowed away, because I had not wanted them to see me land. But when I sprang ashore I knew that she had come to look for me; there were footprints, and I remember that I compared them with arrowheads. I was flattered, too, because she had seemed aloof; I had not known whether she wanted me to come or not. That day she was looking for me, from the top of the wall. I think a gardener must have noticed her there, and betrayed us. Nobody could have discovered us in the willows. It may be that we felt things were to change, because that hour was the most intense experience of my life. . . ." How could he describe to a child like Veria a sensation that went beyond happiness into an unendurable beauty that if prolonged would have seemed like dying? "I have told you all that you can understand," he ended uneasily.

"How do you know?" Valerius looked up, startled by the intensity in Veria's voice. "I am not a child begging for a lullaby. I can understand why your Fabula let you go" (though actually she did not understand at all). "Any of us can love. You act as if you were the emperor himself."

It was not his arrogance, Veria almost said, staring at the water in front of her; it was his stupidity, his blindness. It had burst upon her with terrifying clarity, as she had uttered the words, that since a common danger had united them in the woods, her thoughts had been only of Valerius. Would he never see that she was near and alive, and not a memory nor dream? She would follow him whatever happened. She looked up with a longing, bewildered movement that reminded him of Fabula; and before he realized what he was doing, he had drawn her instinctively into his arms.

Julia sat down on the roughly made seat (it was simply a slab that Mocco had found in the neighbouring field), and looked up at the fountain. The autumn rains would fill the basin to the full, and unless she were here to empty it, it froze. Then on some hot, subsequent day the rim would crack, and in place of the boy with a wolf cub on his shoulder, from whose mouth a jet of water spurted, there would be a broken column, with a nest of shaggy curls for the next season's lizards. According to Mocco, it did not matter whether the water came from a lip or a hole, provided that there was enough for the goats in the evening; but she wondered what the origin of this conflict was, between the barbarians and beauty? Envy perhaps? The fountain gave as much of the source as the trough; both were handmaidens of earth. Yet if Mocco could keep his land, he would be happier under an Alemannic chief than he was under Roman rule. He grudged the wild flowers their few patches of ground, and if he looked at a fruit blossom, it was to inspect it for worms. It was stupid, she knew, to become so attached to inanimate objects; yet as the light caught the statue's knees, and the sun turned the patina into flesh colour, the weather-beaten face seemed to murmur, "Yes, you might have followed Marcus, but we shall stay here, attached to this plinth, till the snows or the summers of the Alemanni topple us under the thistles and grasses."

Aie, Julia thought, pushing back a lock of hair from her forehead, such thoughts were dangerous. If Marcus had wanted to marry her, it was from pity, and not because of her grey hair; though this, and she leaned forward to look at her reflexion in the basin, was not strictly true, she was still almost as dark as her brother was fair. Poor Valerius! They might be raided any evening, yet he still saw her wedded to Marcus, with women scattering flowers! He seemed unable to realize that his own actions had made such a union impossible. Not that she blamed her brother entirely; the woman had caught him in her own skilful trap, and had left him to bear the consequences afterwards; but after the humiliation and the disgrace, after their parents had sold half the Ceresio land for bribes, so that they could get him transferred from Pannonia, Valerius had not uttered a single word of repentance, nor had seemed to understand their sacrifice. His commander's wife! Julia looked at the statue again, and shivered.

There was a trace of Marcus, both in the way that the boy on the fountain seemed to move forward, and in the set of his shoulder under the cub's weight. That was why she liked to sit here, to dream now and again that they might have met when they were young, before the tragedy had happened. Marcus was the only one who had sympathized with her about her father. "Had Valerius no thought for him?" he had asked gravely on the one occasion when they had discussed the affair. They both believed in the same virtues, and wanted the same pattern for their lives. "It is hard to be a Roman," Marcus had continued, and she had known that he was not speaking of himself alone, but was including her in his thought, "but if we keep the laws, they are a wall around us that no enemy can pierce."

It was impossible now; she would not have him take

her out of pity, and it had been pity that had caused their quarrel. He had pretended that her brother's escapade had been forgotten. Besides, she could not leave Orba. Every fibre of her body was rooted to this soil, to the little stream that wandered below them through her dreams and her prayers. There was also Veria. "We, who have inherited the tradition, are bound to transmit it to our descendants." How often she had repeated that proud sentence to the child, without pausing to think that it might have lost its authority in these wild hills. She had only to shut her eyes to hear her father telling her about the majesty of Rome, a city which for Veria hardly existed. In spite of herself, Julia could not help blaming her brother for their poverty. How could she keep her ward secluded in the women's quarters, when there was only an old freedwoman and a couple of slaves to bake, spin, weave and dig? Veria had seemed so young, racing boisterously up the path with a basket of berries, or with a fish dangling from her line, that she had forgotten she was almost at the age when the country girls married. It must be Nennius; there were no other boys in the neighbourhood, and Julia sighed, she did not want to see the girl turn into a drudge in some desolate and lonely outpost.

The ivy was creeping gently towards the wolf. Julia let this grow in summer, "The marble needs the shade as much as we do," but she uprooted it ruthlessly before the gales. Usually it rested her to sit and watch the shadows lengthen across the grass; but today, wherever she turned, some memory mocked her, the sacrifices that she had made turned into dust. She had longed to dedicate herself to Apollo, only to be aware of some rejection; she supposed she had sinned too often. Was it her inability to control her thoughts? These assumed more shapes than tritons in the sea; she could dominate them during her habitual tasks, only to have them mock her while she slept. Why Apollo, people had asked. Apollo was the protector of lawgivers, not of women. It was just for that reason, because she wanted something implacable and austere, instead of the wailing and the incense of the East. She had gone to the Mysteries and had not been saved; she had lied when she had pretended to feel a different being afterwards. Yet Claudia, that foolish girl, who had walked in the procession beside her without knowing the prayers, had drawn an ecstasy from the laurel leaves denied to herself, in spite of fasting and supplication. Aie! What act had she committed that even in front of the altar there had been no forgiveness?

Something rumbled in the distance; Julia sprang to her feet, then she recognized the sound. It was Mocco's wagon jolting over the rough, unmended road. Perhaps the woods were already full of archers? The noise would be the worst, she thought, when the gates slammed, and men rushed to the walls, and the babies cried. Or perhaps the end would come suddenly, with a torch flung on to a thatched roof? She almost wished that she could die here, among the ferns and the fresh pine needles. Yet suppose that she had no time to use her dagger on herself? She seemed to smell cooking fat in a battered cauldron, and see the elderly slave that she might become, stirring and scratching, scratching and stirring, with fleas crawling over her dirty, naked shoulder, and children jeering at her Roman speech. Then she looked up at the fountain again, and tried to murmur, "Let it be as the gods will."

Julia leaned back, and shut her eyes. She would be safe with Marcus, but she was Roman and must not think of safety. What had been the real reason for their quarrel? It had been partly Veria, "The child is no real kin to you, but I will arrange a match with one of my colonists, near enough for you to see her some-times." It had been the word kin, the suggestion that her family was at an end, that had made her lose her temper the following day when he had tried to minimize the extent of her brother's disgrace. There could never be another man as nobly virtuous as her father. Yet Veria, for whom she had been willing to renounce so much, now thought herself in love with a rough, awk-ward boy. Love, Julia pinched the fluff of the dandelion beside her, what had love to do with life or with the gods?

"Sometimes I think, Julia, that you evade your re-sponsibilities because of some scruple," Marcus had said. "Most women can spin, but it is given to few to be able to organize a great household." Yet she ought to have been a priestess; had she not spoiled her life by acceptance of that first marriage at her father's command? She owed her parents obedience; why had no vision come to convince them that her destiny lay in the temple rather than the home? "I have had nothing," she murmured to the statue, "nothing." Then she turned quickly towards the orchard, because she could almost hear Marcus mocking her again, "Use the gifts that the gods have given you, instead of questioning them. Then you will be happy."

The sun had set. There were voices between the trees. Valerius was walking up the hill, with his arm round Veria's shoulder. In that remote spot they supposed themselves alone. "Promise me that I can stay with you," Veria was pleading. "If Domina Julia knows that I love you, she will send me away."

Julia stopped. They both looked so happy, but the girl was purely Helvetian, there was no trace in her manner of Roman restraint. "It may be for the best," Julia muttered; she felt too weary and too lonely to interfere. She stepped on to the path because it was better that they should see her, and said with cold resignation, "I was mistaken, Valerius. I should not have sent the boy to Aventicum; you ought to have gone there yourself."

III

<hr style="border: 2px solid black;">

Aventicum. July

"AN official! An official is asking for you." The inn-keeper himself had waddled rapidly across the yard to a bench where Demetrius was inspecting some harness. "It is the governor's own steward," he hissed, a mixture of greed and curiosity on his face, as the trader turned to face him.

Demetrius had never seen his mules in better condition. They had feasted long enough in the Alpine pastures near Orba for their flanks to become glossy without getting fat. "Check every buckle," he ordered, "and take whatever needs repair to Rufus. He is the best harness maker in the empire. Felix will show you where he lives." He wiped his hands on a cloth, handed it back to his servant, and followed the innkeeper to the front courtyard. Such a summons was always alarming. It was probable that it was merely an order to show his wares at the governor's villa, before they were offered for general sale; but in these times there were so many regulations that he might have broken one involuntarily, and then, in spite of his care in bribing the guard when they had entered Aventicum, he would be assessed at double the rate. In any event, it was important that this crafty thief should notice no anxiety, he had already charged the trader an outrageous price for oats; so they walked together in complete silence towards the visitor.

A tall figure in a white tunic was pacing up and down the little garden. A small fair-haired boy followed him with a fly whisk, stopping whenever his master stopped, to swish it through the air. The steward had buried his nose in a small sprig of aromatic mountain bush that was also reputed to keep away flies. He turned haughtily when he heard their footsteps, and waited for the trader to approach him. "There is some report that you have spices," he began; then they stared at each other and he exclaimed, almost incredulously, "Why, Demetrius! What are you doing here? I thought the pirates had captured you long ago, if you had not become one yourself!"

"Thallus! No, I gave up the sea. One voyage cured me of the ocean for life. Not that the land is any safer. Some of your barbarians shot at me a few weeks ago, not so many miles away, at Saltus."

"Saltus! But that is just above Orba."

"I know. The garrison rescued me, but I got an arrow through my shoulder. Aie, it still smarts."

"A good season will be a salve for it," Thallus answered complacently. "Come now, what have you really got in your sacks? Because we learnt our ciphers together on the same potsherd is not a reason to open the governor's house to you, unless you have something of value."

"You can judge for yourself. I will get my men to undo the bales. I have amber, and a fur garment such as I have never touched in ten years of wandering. The governor of Vindonissa wanted to buy it from me, but I heard that your master had a taste in cloaks, so I brought it here to show to him. There are very few unguents. It's the plague in Egypt. Hardly any ships have reached us from the East."

"It's for his lady," Thallus grunted.

"I have still a few phials, both Syrian and Egyptian; but while my slaves fetch them, let me offer you a drink. I have one flask left of real, smoke-dried Rhaetian."

"Not wine. It's my liver," Thallus clasped his hands in front of his tunic. "But my master is occupied this evening, and I am at liberty. Come and dine with me at a cooler and less frequented inn than this, and we can look at the phials on our return. I will take your word about the cloak and the amber; it will be useless showing these to him until after the Games."

Demetrius sighed, and the two Greeks nodded at each other.

"It may be a good thing for the sausage vendors," the merchant grumbled, "but it is bad for my business. People wager their silver upon the flick of an arm; if they win, they drink the coins up in a night, and if they lose, why, they haven't enough to buy a comb for their wives."

"And there will be no work done in the town for days," Thallus echoed gloomily. He lifted his aromatic shrub to the straight nose that seemed part of his forehead, as if the air were already polluted. A donkey brayed from the neighbouring stable, while a group of peasants came tramping across the stones in hobnailed sandals. "Shall we go?" Thallus asked.

Demetrius looked round; Felix, his freedman, appeared at his elbow. It was extraordinary how the man seemed to know everything, so that he was always there to anticipate every need. Yet in spite of this service he was a surly, discontented fellow whom nobody liked. "Shall I tell my man to bring the perfumes over to us?" the trader asked. "It would save you from having to return here."

"Yes, if they will not take long to unpack. I can leave my boy, Aristo, here. He knows the way. And now, tell me about Verona." Thallus started off with such long strides that Demetrius almost had to run to keep up with him. "I suppose the city has completely changed?"

His friend knew how to look after himself, the trader thought, looking around the shady garden that resembled a wealthy citizen's summer villa more than an inn. The tables had been set under the trees, and although there were a couple of groups at the opposite end from where they reclined, there was a discreet space between them, and neither music nor women. "As a traveller who knows his way about, permit me to congratulate you, Thallus. I have not been in such pleasant surroundings since I left Verona."

The steward bowed almost haughtily, as if it were his due. "We tire of pomp and long for a little simplicity. Still, I must admit that it was a long time before I found the place; the host cooks himself, and only for guests he knows; he will scarcely admit strangers."

"From Croton, I suppose; they say the best cooks come from there."

"Oddly enough, no. He is a native of Aventicum. The gods gave him this grace, I imagine, and a feeling for his material. He never uses other than the local produce. Of course, in the old days, when we were on the main road to Lugdunum, they called the city a capital of cook shops."

"It is a sign of prosperity," Demetrius said, wiping his lips. The light was fading out of the sky, but there was a slight breeze for the first time in a week. A leaf or two stirred on the chestnut tree, and the air was cool.

"Your man, will he be much longer, do you think?" Thallus asked, looking across at the entrance.

"Felix never wastes time, but perfumes have become so scarce that I keep them locked and always under

68

guard. It frightens me to think about Egypt; I pray the plague does not reach us here."

Thallus shivered. "We have good air, if we are a provincial backwater. There is much to be said for a little town that is too quiet to be envied either by the legions or the emperor."

"You have done well for yourself," Demetrius answered in a flattering voice, though he knew privately that he would not be inside his friend's tunic for its weight in gold. What had Thallus done with his eyes and ears? In a year, or perhaps two, the tribes would sweep forward, and even if Aventicum survived unpillaged, the surrounding land and its trade would be utterly destroyed.

"I have tried to follow the philosophers," Thallus answered gravely. "All that matters is my duty. It has been hard to accept the burden at times, with this miserable liver I inherited, if you remember, from my father, but the governor has been pleased to reward me with his confidence." Thallus smoothed, with a prim gesture, the folds of his tunic. "You must excuse my informal dress," he added, "but the toga at midsummer here really is too warm."

It was not surprising to see his friend in an official position. Many schools had shut, and it was often difficult to find a man who could cipher at all. "I wish the frontiers were safer," Demetrius said cautiously, after a moment.

"The men who attacked you were escaped slaves, or

69

robbers," Thallus answered indifferently. "You have not seen my boy?" he asked, as a serving girl put a dish of fresh mountain trout in front of each of them. She shook her head, as if she were afraid to speak, and Thallus continued, "Aristo likes fish; I hope he comes before it gets cold."

"The men who shot me were Alemanni; we found some arrowheads."

"Some outlaw, I expect; oh, Aristo, you rascal, where have you been lingering, I suppose you forgot dinner." Thallus drove his knife into the cavity below the fish's eye, dipped the flake in butter, and placed it gently between the boy's lips. "The Emperor Vitellius dined only on the cheeks of trout," he added.

"He must have needed hundreds." Demetrius looked up at Felix who had a basket swinging from his arm, and a sack over his shoulder. "Ah, you brought the cloak, I see; that is excellent, I want my friend's opinion of it."

Thallus was caressing Aristo's head. "It is useless showing the governor anything before the Games."

"I am showing this to you, not to the governor. You will appreciate it. Feel the softness of that skin, go over it hair by hair, there isn't a mark or blemish anywhere."

Thallus dried his fingers on a napkin and stroked the garment that Felix spread in front of him. "By Hercules, you are right," he looked at his friend with a grudging admiration, "and how it would suit my shoulders on a winter day. Are you offering it to me as a gift?" he laughed.

"In exchange for Aristo?" Demetrius teased.

"Ah no, I couldn't exchange this rascal for a cloak, though he is my own slave, bought last spring, for I will not whisper how many sesterces. No, child, leave it alone"; he gave the boy, who was trying to wrap the fur around himself, a playful pat. "You had better fold it up, Felix, before any butter gets spilt on it. But after these wretched Games are over, I will see that you are summoned to the governor."

Demetrius bowed. "Leave the basket, Felix, but take the cloak back with you, and send a man to wait for me at the door." Then he turned to the fish, dipping each morsel in the rich sauce, and eating it slowly, because he could seldom afford trout, and they had been particularly scarce and expensive this year.

"I have only the usual perfumes," the trader said lazily, after picking the last bones bare, "is it only for a lady, or are they wanted for a feast after the Games?"

"It's for his woman." Thallus almost spat out the words.

"Oh, that is easy, they all like myrrh. I think I have got what you want, but with your permission, I will show it to you after this excellent meal is finished." Thallus nodded assent; he had been giving most of his trout to Aristo, who was sitting beside him, cross-legged, on the pavement. "I have ordered you a little lamb, Demetrius; they have a way of cooking it with mountain herbs that all my friends enjoy. For myself," and he clasped his tunic again with the same convulsive gesture, "I can only play with some lettuce leaves. My physician has forbidden me meat."

"If it had not been for the trout, I should have suspected you of being a follower of Epicurus. What strange fellows they are! They claim liberty for their pleasures, and then live on pulse."

"I have studied the sayings, of course, and agree with many of them, but it's a harsh doctrine; a man is to be indifferent to heat or cold, to good fortune or bad, and then have no reward even when he is dead. I prefer the Mysteries myself. You are interested in philosophy?" Thallus added eagerly.

"As a wayfarer, I am interested in everything," Demetrius grunted. A panorama seemed to unfold as he spoke: that slave girl, she might have been Thetis, on the old harbour wall, holding up a shell to his ear; long dusty roads; the curious barbarian faces looking from the amulet that was his pass into their camp, to the bundle of daggers that he had brought in to sell to them. "I feel sometimes that life is chance, then a thread appears, but never in a straight line; it knots itself, twists, you lose it again . . ."

"I know that there is some plan," Thallus selected a crisp leaf, and held it up to the light to be sure that it was free from flies. "It ought to be like the ciphers on my tablets, tall, and in regular pattern; instead we destroy it through our foolishness."

72

"We are far from perfection, especially in these less than imperial days," Demetrius helped himself lavishly to the lamb, "or are we? Suppose such thoughts are only runaway horses, and this is the summation," he lifted up a portion of meat, "with a cool evening, and our meeting again after so many years."

Thallus permitted himself to smile. "I am still grateful to you for beating off those urchins who were pelting us with fish skins."

"But you did my sums for me."

"Yes, how long ago it seems; life began for me after I arrived in Aventicum."

"If it had not been for Valerius, I should not be here to remind you of your childhood. I enjoyed those days myself, on the whole."

"Yes, child," Thallus nodded, "go and play until they bring the fruit.

"What grace," he murmured, as Aristo's thin, brown legs flashed across the courtyard. "You were saying? Yes, the man at Orba is a good soldier. He might have been the governor of Raurica, if it had not been for a woman."

"He has no woman now, except his sister, not even a slave girl, though I tried to sell him one."

"I am glad you were unsuccessful. They are the root of our troubles." Thallus examined a speck on the leaf he held, and flung it on to the ground. "My master treats me as if I were his friend; he is an excellent official, and exact in his accounts. Yet he wastes his silver on an aging companion, who has not even a youthful complexion to commend her; they quarrel, and then he drinks."

"So I have heard in the town," Demetrius nodded gravely.

"You are not married?"

"I am a merchant. Like yourself, Thallus, first I saved to add to my team of mules; then I put a few pieces by, to purchase a bit of land. The roads are not easy, and I am no longer the urchin I was, when we chased butterflies together, nor even the man of five years ago who could walk twenty miles and drive a bargain before he slept. I used to say that if I gained any silver on my final journey, I would buy myself a Lydian; then I saw a woman once, the priestess of a temple in the mountains, and there was something so merciful and yet majestic about her that I have never wanted a slave since. Believe me, I felt as awkward in her presence as if the Empress herself had summoned me. And then, look at the times, the tolls we have to pay, the bribes to officials! If I get back, with a whole skin, to my olives, I shall be thankful enough to find some old woman to cook for me. As for the rest," he shrugged his shoulders, "it's gold, Thallus; philosophy comes down to that basic fact in the end. Liberty, meat, even the blanket that covers you depend on this," and he slapped down a coin on the table.

"Perhaps you have found the right mistress."

"Yes, but I wonder how much longer the roads will

74

be open? There is too much unrest on the other side of the Rhine."

"You traders only see the dust under your sandals, and not the larger issues of the Empire."

Demetrius bit his lips. You fool, he thought, you have never spoken to a barbarian in your life; you do not know how near the flood is to you. "So you believe that there is no danger of invasion?" he asked innocently.

"Invasion!" Thallus snorted. "For your own sake, Demetrius, I must warn you not to spread rumours. My master takes repressive measures against reckless talk. How is it possible to suppress all robbery in those wild hills? Some men in the last village that you passed warned the outlaws about you. I agree with you that we need more men in the frontier posts, but look at our administrative costs! They rise continually; last year's harvest was good, there were tolls and levies, yet the Treasury is almost empty. All the same, three or four men, who may snatch up a herd boy or a couple of sheep, are different from an army."

The soldiers thought differently at Vindonissa. The truth nearly slipped from the merchant's mouth, but why spoil the evening with an argument; here was the girl again with a great country cheese, and Aristo hopping forward for his share. "Tell me more about Valerius," he said, "the man was kind to me."

"Dozens of officers come in from the outposts every season, to get their pay, see their friends and go to the baths; unless they are invited to dine with the governor, I have nothing to do with them. I remember Valerius because eleven years ago we arrived at Aventicum together."

"Together?"

"If you remember, when my father died, his brother, who was at the Treasury here, sent for me. I was full of a stupid idea then that I wanted to go to Athens, the 'violet-crowned,' you know, and full of philosophers. So I set off hopefully, meaning to live here on bread and water until I had saved enough to continue my studies. After I had been on the road for a month, I had learnt the first doctrine they teach, by painful experience. All I wanted was shade and a quiet corner."

"They say that each journey takes a year from one's life."

"It was one of those minor evils that turn out to have been a blessing in disguise. I was so happy to see my uncle that I settled to work immediately. He was an excellent teacher and I, if I may say so, was an apt pupil. Before he died, he recommended me to the governor. I have never left Aventicum in all these years, except to go occasionally into the hills, after a fever."

"And Valerius?"

"He joined our party, a few days before our arrival here. He was being transferred from Pannonia, through influence, I heard. His father must have owned a lot of land. Originally he had been sent to the Ister as a punishment. Not many officers came back from there alive."

"Why, some conspiracy?"

"No, women again. The fool was discovered in the arms of his commander's wife, in the man's own garden."

"I blame him less for the woman than for being discovered," Demetrius chuckled; "he's used to having his own way, he would be scornful of precautions."

"Women are worse than mildew on a vine. If it had not been for them, my master would have been transferred last year to Mediolanum; there is such a big library there. And your Valerius would be governor of Raurica. It is fortunate that you have no wife."

"And that you confine yourself to Aristo," Demetrius said slyly. Thallus was feeding the boy as if he were a puppy, with dried fruit dipped in honey.

"Could anyone be more charming?" The steward patted the boy's head once more. "However, my real love is for my ciphers. The child amuses me and nothing more. Ouch," Thallus looked down at his leg, "that was more than a mosquito."

"If you are tired of me," Aristo said, his eyes flashing, "Quintus Flavius needs a messenger."

"He is jealous, you see," Thallus rubbed his pinched calf, "but no, child, you are too young to understand what I mean. Here, take this," he handed him a coin, "and ask them in the kitchen to find you some berries."

The boy strode off sulkily, and the trader continued, "But Valerius, you have not told me how you came to know him."

77

"As you can imagine, I was frightened. I had not seen my uncle since I was a baby; and although I rode part of the way on a mule, the long climb over the cold pass almost killed me." Demetrius noticed again the clutching, compulsive gesture. "I was sitting in the courtyard at dusk, the day after we reached the valley, because I could not bear to remain with a dozen snoring muleteers—the smell, you know . . ." Thallus wrinkled up his nose—"when Valerius came up to me. 'What's the matter?' he asked, as gently as if he were my father. Then do you know what he did? He let me sleep in a corner of his room."

"His sister looked after Felix and myself for a week."

"I shall always remember what he said to me. 'Each day is a gift of heaven, of the gods.' I think of this sometimes, when I am alone with my ciphers."

It must have been hard, Demetrius thought, for Thallus to have crossed the Alps. He had been too delicate as a boy to join the others in their games, and the stinging comments that he had made about his companions, though often true, had earned him many enemies.

"Some wine," Thallus said, rousing himself, as the innkeeper came towards them. "I shall join you for once, if I have to pay for it tomorrow." He glanced uneasily towards the kitchen, but Aristo had disappeared.

How lonely he seemed. Demetrius cut off a last, small sliver of the cheese and said, hoping to distract his friend, "You have had much experience. Tell me, what is going to happen to the Empire?"

Thallus shrugged his shoulders. "It depends from what angle you look at it. If a farmer hears that the tribes are over the frontier, he thinks about his flocks. Rome herself is powerful enough to bear a few scratches. Or let me explain it this way: I let Aristo take liberties with me here, as my master might let his hunting dog nibble his fingers, but in the daytime, when there is work to be done, boy and dog are banished. It is a bad moment, I agree, at present. We have not got the right ruler."

"He may have deprived the senators of some of their power, but even his enemies agree that Gallien is a soldier. Think of what he has done since his father was taken prisoner on that disastrous expedition into Asia. He put down the rebellion in Illyria, and has defeated the barbarians in Gaul."

"I will tell you something," Thallus leaned forward, and his eyes glittered maliciously, "but it is for your ears only, remember, not the market place."

"You can trust me," Demetrius answered, "my business depends upon my discretion." This was not strictly true, but the trader prided himself upon being careful as to place; it was a foolish chattering in front of slaves that was harmful.

"The Empress is a Christian."

"A Christian!" Even Demetrius was startled, trained as he was to conceal his feelings.

79

"Secretly. Of course, this makes it worse."

"And the Emperor? He repealed his father's edict against them as soon as he came to power, but I never like persecution, it robs me of customers."

"It is sometimes necessary." Aristo bounded back from the kitchen and sat down at his master's feet. Thallus smiled, chose a plum from the small heap in front of him, and held it out for the child to bite.

"They usually arrest the wrong people."

The sky was so deep a blue that it seemed black, and so strung with stars that Demetrius remembered an African he had seen, walking in a procession, with a necklace of small quartz stones hanging over his black chest. It was much cooler, and apart from a murmur of conversation, almost silent. "I cannot understand it," Thallus continued, "because the Emperor is a friend of the philosophers, and the Christians continually attack them."

"I grudge no man his gods, but the Christians want to sweep away all those who do not agree with them. One of my men belongs to the sect; he is a good worker, but a joyless fellow, and so stubborn. Not that I like the other new ideas from Asia, either. But has the Empress much influence, do you suppose?"

Thallus shrugged his shoulders again. "The influence of any woman is beyond human measurement. She is that tiny fraction we omit to count, that throws the reckoning into chaos afterwards. In my opinion, an Emperor should reign alone."

Demetrius nodded. "You think there may be changes soon?" he enquired.

"How should I know? We are safer at Aventicum than in the cities nearer Rome. If a ruler dies, and Gallien has many enemies, the officials sweep away the people they dislike, in order, they pretend, to secure the purple for his successor. We may not be as important as in the days when the town was Vespasian's cradle, but we have our cornfields and our vineyards, and we are not famous enough to be envied. Besides, feel how cool it is," Thallus continued, "the heat of the last days has been insupportable. Even if your famous barbarians besiege us, my roots are too deep in this soil for me to leave. I could never bear that southern heat again that I remember from my childhood."

"There is not much difference between Verona and here."

"Except the trifle that I have just mentioned, my roots. They go down as deep as a well. Apart from my health, I have been happy here."

Demetrius stifled a yawn, and leaned over to tighten his sandals. It was light enough to see their way; they would not need a torch. The guests had departed, other than three young men who were strolling towards the door. One of the three, a broad-shouldered youth, with the dark eyes and thick hair of a southerner, left his companions and greeted Thallus. "This is Gallio," the steward said, "born here, though his father came from Narbonensis. He is our one and only painter."

81

"I have done nothing, nothing . . ." Gallio looked at Demetrius mournfully, "I have never been outside Aventicum."

"You cannot sweep the centuries away with your brush. The paintings in our temple to Apollo are most beautiful."

"But they do not express what people are thinking today! Oh yes, I know, my curves are less serene than those on the wall; and I know the pictures are magnificent, I have grown up looking at them. But I shall lose what vision I have, if I continue to repeat what has been painted a dozen times already. I want to go to Rome."

"We have forgotten the lessons of the Golden Age. It would be better to remember them."

"No," Gallio shook his head and his fingers seemed to curl round an invisible brush, "I want my pictures to move. Have you noticed that even a sleeping child is never still, that the dust shivers, though this may be simply the light on it, and all we do is to cover a surface with patterns."

"He has been learning oratory from some strolling rhetorician," Thallus said smiling. "Patience, Gallio, we all behave strangely in summer."

"I like the heat," Gallio answered indignantly; then, though his fists were clenched, he checked himself. "Has the governor . . . ?"

"No, nor have I any intention of speaking to him before the Games are over. Make a sacrifice to Fortune,

Gallio; your luck depends upon a throw of the dice. If my master wins his wagers, he will have money and be in a good humour; then I can show him the plaster flaking from the wall, and suggest that we repair the atrium. Till then, his answer would be a plain and angry No."

"I would do it for little more than the cost of my paints, and my food."

"Impatient child! It all depends on the dice, but you know I will help you if I can."

"My friends are waiting," Gallio said; he bowed in a ceremonious, old-fashioned way that was in such sharp contrast to his rebellious words that Demetrius smiled. The boy mistook this for some secret understanding between them, and was about to speak, but the trader said hurriedly, feeling a subtle irritation in the air, "Show me your paintings some time." Then he added, turning to his friend, "Alas, as they say, good things contain their end. We have work to do in the morning; I fear I must return to my inn."

"Farewell." Gallio bowed again; he moved more quickly than the Helvetians, Demetrius thought, as he watched him run after his companions. It was too dark now to see more than the outline of the trees, but Thallus grunted, almost before the painter was out of earshot, "It's sad. The boy has talent but he is a fool. He married."

Demetrius stifled a second yawn; he had no particular interest in paintings. "What an evening! I have never been so happy for years. In spite of your roots, Thallus, I wish you lived in Verona, not too far from my olives."

"We must meet again, after the Games." Thallus sighed; he had drunk too much, he knew, there was a sharp pain beginning in the familiar place, although the single carefully sipped cup would have been a mere mouthful to any of his acquaintances. He bent down and woke Aristo gently; the boy had been asleep on a straw mat beside his feet for the last half hour. The innkeeper appeared as if a thought had summoned him, and though Demetrius politely turned his head away, his trained eyes noticed the size of the coin that the steward slipped into the cook's hand.

"I'm a plain man," Demetrius said, "and I can only give plain thanks. This is the moment when I would willingly borrow phrases from Gallio's orator, except that my tongue would trip over saying them," and they both laughed.

"The greatest art is simplicity, and that, I fear, is something our young painter will never learn. But the phials: I hate to spoil this last moment with a matter of trade, only the governor sent me to you, and early tomorrow morning he will stamp in, asking for the perfumes."

Demetrius had shaken his man awake, and was already lifting a couple of straw-wrapped jars from the basket. "This is for yourself," he said, pressing a tiny phial into his friend's hand, "it's old but good, like ourselves! And this," he held up a squat jar with a slight grimace, "is the myrrh that they always like, in a new bottle. It should solve your master's difficulties for the moment. No, I want nothing for either of them; if Fortune smiles on Vinodius, ask him later to let me show him my furs." The perfumes were more costly than a banquet, but it was worth making a sacrifice if he could sell the governor that cloak.

In the moonlight the solitary column that the peasants called the Stork (there was some legend that a pair had nested on it) tapered into the sky as if it were made from foam, and not marble. It was a lighthouse, Thallus thought, a *pharos;* though Aventicum was not Alexandria, and the waves here were green, sweeping up in a circle of broken meadows. "You will see," he said aloud, because they had come as far as the crossroads where their paths divided, "this is no frontier town. We have preserved a pure form of the imperial tradition, just because we are isolated and humble. If your barbarians reach our gates, which I very much doubt, it will be to kneel and pay us the tribute of their wonder."

"Perhaps," Demetrius said doubtfully, rubbing his shoulder.

"Sell your olives and come and settle with us; you will pay only half the taxes."

"Tonight, now we have found each other again, why even speak of parting?"

Thallus seemed almost storklike himself, as with one hand on Aristo's shoulder, he lifted the other in farewell. "Till after the Games," Demetrius called, turning down the lane that led to his lodging. How late it was! He hoped it would not be too difficult to wake the watchman and get him to unbar the door. And how strange it was that nothing altered; now he was afraid of the innkeeper, but in their boyhood after they had chattered too long on the way back from school, they had tried to avoid meeting their fathers.

Demetrius walked slowly up the deserted road. Thallus had not changed. He was still the boy who had muffled himself up in a cloak until midsummer, and who had refused to meet the mule teams coming in from Rome. Still, perhaps it was only a traveller like himself who could appreciate to the full such an unexpected meeting with a half-forgotten friend, in the middle of an alien town. Then he wondered if the Emperor had married a Christian, and if this were as important as Thallus believed? What the Empire needed was a good commander, and Gallien looked after his soldiers, even if he were otherwise, as they said, strange and cruel. What was this flaw that was spreading across the land? He contrasted the evening, its conversation, its tranquillity, with that terrifying hour that he had spent in a hiding place of the barbarians, on the Roman side of the Rhine. He had gone there by invitation, because they had wanted his goods, and if they had stabbed him, no other trader would have gone there afterwards. But they had been more like giants than men, sitting half naked round the fire, with scars of claw marks over their bodies; and he looked up now at the fragile columns of a terrace opposite him, and sighed. It was the tolls, he decided; people stayed in their villages, and did not know what was happening twenty leagues away. Or was it something beyond all this that he could not even imagine? He shrugged his shoulders, turned, but Thallus had disappeared; only the wind seemed to echo a faint cry of parting, through the muffled leaves.

IV

—————————

TULLIA yawned. Summer in Aventicum was really insupportable. There had always been a sea breeze in her native Genua. "Careful, Secunda," she snapped, and the slave who was dressing her hair looked up with frightened eyes. "The pins slip so in the heat," the girl murmured, wiping a bone ornament with a cloth.

Tullia did not reply. She prided herself upon treating her slaves well; a beating only made their hands tremble, besides, it was no longer fashionable. She had trained Secunda to her ways, and with the price that they asked at present for a hairdresser, she knew that she was fortunate to have such a servant. She picked up her mirror and inspected the curls; on the whole, the result was successful.

"I hear they are combing the hair back at Mediolanum," Tullia said, "and dressing it quite simply."

"So plain a style is not for my lady, with her thick and beautiful hair." Very skilfully, Secunda twisted another ringlet into place.

Tullia nodded. She felt both melancholy and irritable.

Vinodius had suddenly become so difficult. Twice, when he should have come to her, he had made an excuse. It was partly this matter of the Games, and at the very thought of them she yawned again. Latin as she was, she had no desire to see a man roll over dead in the stench of the arena (there were other purposes in life for him), nor swagger up to the barrier, all scars and brawn. The circus was different. Oh, any woman could fall in love with the charioteers as they guided their plunging horses round the turn, the blue or the green reins whipping like grass snakes round their tall bodies. But there was no circus at Aventicum; it had been three years since they had even had a company of players in the town; more and more people drifted south, and the place was rapidly becoming a mere village as she remarked to Vinodius whenever he became too pompous. "Did you ever see Hesperius?" she asked; and Secunda smiled, a pleading, hopeful smile that begged forgiveness for the heat of the afternoon, the pins slipping, and the bad temper of her mistress. "I have never been outside Aventicum, my lady."

"He belonged to the Blues," Tullia continued; it pleased her to while away this dreary time of day by recalling the memory aloud. "I was very young. I ought not to have been at the circus at all, but my brother had taken me as a reward. I had brought him a message from one of my friends, a girl with the longest hair I have ever seen, and such a strange colour; it was almost red. Ah me, I wonder what became of her?" This was pure invention because Tullia had actually gone with her first lover, the prosperous owner of a fish shop, but she had told her own version of the day so often that she had come to believe in the truth of it herself. "Everybody was betting upon the Greens, but I was just a child, I made no wager." Tullia sighed; it really *was* a very long time ago. "Oh, you should have seen the parade at the starting line. Each group had its emblem, and Hesperius stood there, with his fingers on the reins, as if they had been not leather but a girl's flying ribbons. He leaned forward once to speak to his horses. Otherwise, in all that movement, he was absolutely still. I saw the praetor drop his handkerchief, the chariots bounded down the course, earth and sea, the Green and the Blue, storms rising in the mountain, surf rushing up the sand at night." Tullia sighed again; she longed to be back in Genua. "I have never cared to look at statues since, they disappoint me."

Secunda listened avidly, a bone pin in her mouth. She had often heard the tale before, but she liked stories; besides, if her mistress were thinking about something else, there was less risk of an angry word if her thumb caught in a strand of hair. "And he won?" she asked, at the appropriate moment, taking the pin out of her mouth, and slipping it into a roll above Tullia's ear.

"He won. Women threw him their bracelets, before his horses, they were Numidian, I believe, had their hoofs fully over the line. That is the end of the course; they mark it in white on the sand. I shall never forget how the crowd roared. He looked up at us and laughed, and waved his whip. Then the owner of the chariot gave him a banquet."

"He cannot have been as handsome as my master," Secunda ventured shyly, and her mistress smiled. Her slave's worship of Vinodius amused her. "Of course not, child. How can we compare a charioteer with a Roman governor?"

She had had no bracelet then to throw to Hesperius, only perhaps a heart. Yet a change in her own fortunes dated from that day. She had noticed how quietly the wives of the tribunes had sat in their seats; and later, when she had left the fish-shop owner for the arms of a young officer, she had not embarrassed him with importunate begging or noisy behaviour. The officer had been recalled to Rome, but had recommended her to a friend of his; it had happened to be Vinodius, whose wife she had been, except for the mere name, for the past nine years. "I often saw him race," she said, as Secunda stepped aside to sprinkle a little perfume over the now finished curls, "and then, we came here. I forgot about the circus until one day an officer came from Genua. We pressed him for the news and he told us a dozen stories about why the price of tunny fish had risen, as if that mattered to us when we never see it here. Then, just as I was about to withdraw, because they were bringing round the wine, he said as if it had no importance at all, 'Hesperius, the charioteer, was killed the other day.' Aie! I wept."

"Aie!" the maid echoed, she had the peasant girl's capacity to throw herself into the mood of any story. "Aie! How sad!"

"Yes, the officer said that one of the Greens had managed to loosen the axle pin of a wheel, and the chariot overturned a few yards from the finish. Like Adonis, the boy died young, and Aphrodite must have grieved for him; yet," Tullia put her hand on the mirror but did not lift it up, "he had had his five years, everything that he wanted, and the love of thousands. Perhaps it was easier to have the swift and sudden end."

"But it is always sad to die young," the maid persisted.

From the shadows it was almost sunset, but the ointments on the low black table smelled rancid in the heat. The little jars in the centre completely covered the painting of the three nymphs dancing before Apollo. There was not much space, but Tullia refused to dress in her own room; Vinodius had a habit of strolling in suddenly for a moment, and there was nothing that a man disliked more than the smell of oils and the sight of paints. She looked disconsolately at the phial that held the Egyptian perfume that her lover liked so much, and noticed that it was almost empty. "Is it true that there is a Greek merchant in the town? I need more of those Egyptian scents."

"I will find out," Secunda answered cautiously; she prided herself upon not listening to the gossip of the household. It was safer for her if the other servants knew that she never carried tales about them to her mistress.

How tiresome it was that the Empire was so unsettled! Tullia took the stopper out of the bottle and held it up to her nose. The Syrian who had sold it to her had said that there was magic in it, and the heavy, aromatic scent wafted her miles away from this isolated, sleepy province. It was naturally the usual trading chatter, but the oil had seemed to please Vinodius. Ever since she had had to be miserly with it, because there was hardly a drop left, he had neglected her to go and drink with his brother officers, and quarrel over the merits of rival swordsmen whose names she had never even heard. "There was a girl in Genua," she continued, as Secunda began to rub the spare combs with a rag, "and she told me that in Bithynia, where she was born, there was a great festival when they carried roses to the temple, and every woman had a new robe."

Secunda began to put the extra pins away in a long, red earthenware dish. I wish she would stop clattering, Tullia thought, and yawned. It would be easy to buy any perfume that she wanted in the south. Vinodius had known the Emperor; why had he lost the promotion to Mediolanum in the previous spring? Simply because nobody remembered them in this backwater, they were wasting their lives; presently they would be old. She picked her mirror up idly, and gasped. Instead of a pyramid of curls above a pair of smooth cheeks, a wrinkled face was staring at her, with hollow eyes, and the bitter, weather-eaten lines of a mask of the Fates. She clutched the handle, sprang to the light; the features now were less drawn than they had seemed to be in the shadow, but could this be her? There was fear in the eyes, something had happened to the lips. She opened her mouth to scream, the movement was reflected back to her. "Quick, girl, a cloth," she panted, "this heat is making me faint."

"I think my lady worries too much about the soothsayer," Secunda said, putting a wet towel at the back of Tullia's neck. "He said he saw change, but change is not necessarily evil. Besides, there is a new man in the town, if my lady would care to consult him?"

"It is what they say when the auguries are not fortunate," Tullia moaned. She was beyond the aid of soothsayers. Had those curious eyes seen her, not as she was now, the most powerful woman in Aventicum, but as she might be in a year, living with a single slave in the outskirts of Genua? If Vinodius were tired . . . she trembled, she tried to pretend that it was only the heat, but nothing helped. A chasm had opened between her life of only that morning and this hour.

It was then, in the middle of the turmoil, while she was still so frightened that she was shivering in spite of the hot afternoon, that Vinodius knocked. She could not check a little scream as he entered. "I see you are not expecting me," he teased, "are you waiting for your lover, or a soothsayer?"

"Vinodius!" Tullia rose—it was comforting to have

him tease her—and walked into the large adjoining room. She nodded, and Secunda left, with the ointment box under her arm. The girl ventured to look up at the governor as she passed him, and Vinodius smiled back.

"I know! It would be hard to be unfaithful to me in Aventicum. If I leave a slice of meat on my plate, the beggar boys are discussing whether it was because of stomach ache, or poison, before I get up from the table."

"Couldn't we go back to Genua this winter? It is eight years since I have seen a city."

"But this is the capital of a province," he protested. He picked up the thin linen robe, with the Syrian embroidery, that Secunda had spread out for her mistress, and looked at his broad fingers under the transparent stuff as if it were a mirror. "Still, you are right; it is time we had a holiday, only it will have to be next spring."

Tullia pouted. If she could fill her lungs with the sea breezes of her native town, the black despair of the last half hour might vanish. "Promise me that you will not wager too many farms on the wrong swordsman?"

Vinodius leaned down and pinched the back of her neck. "Oh," she gave a little affected cry, "I am not one of your hunting puppies. It will show tomorrow."

"What does it matter, if you are not going to attend the Games?" Actually he was delighted that Tullia never wished to appear with him in public. He had taken her once to the races soon after they had met, and could still remember with jealous mortification the look that she had given some wretched charioteer, a pole of a man, with a blue fillet round his hair, looking more like an actor than a racer. He kissed Tullia, and added, "It's true, it is no longer fashionable for women to be seen at the arena."

"Men are so cruel," Tullia cooed. "When I feed my pigeons in the morning, it makes me cry if one bird takes a crumb away from the other."

"I never think about birds, unless I eat them."

"Ouch!" She gave another little scream. Had she been boastful? How had she offended the gods? She had waited for Vinodius minute after minute for a week. Now he had come when she wanted to be alone and collect her thoughts; there was no surer way to lose a lover than to be melancholy in his arms. Vinodius had begun to walk restlessly up and down. What was she thinking of? Oh, a game that girls had always played in Genua, kneeling round a fountain, to watch the reflections. A breath, the clouds would blow away, there would be blue sky, almost a feeling of youth waiting for her. Let this darkness disperse, she prayed; it only needed a touch, but nothing happened. Then she stammered desperately, because Vinodius had his hand on the curtain that hung over the doorway, "Is it true that the Alemanni are being more troublesome than usual this year?"

"Now I know. It was a soothsayer, or else a merchant. I thought you were too intelligent to listen to gossip."

"Ask your steward. I have seen no one," she answered truthfully. "Only this morning, when I was feeding my birds, I remembered how many tribes there were, and I could not help wondering if they could slip into the town on a winter night. . . ."

"On wings, no doubt. The gods settled that matter permanently, I believe."

"You must not blame me for being afraid." She lifted her arm with all the heavy bracelets that he had given her, and drew his rather reluctant head towards her.

"I have seen the merchant, if you have been virtuous"; he slipped away from her embrace, "don't use too much, it is strong and very scarce." He put the phial that Thallus had brought him into her hands.

"Oh!" She sank to her knees, and pretended to be a slave girl, thanking him for a cake. They laughed and opened the bottle together, and she poured a little into the palm of her hand. If it were the Egyptian perfume, it would be a sign that she was not bewitched, and that the chill that was creeping up and down her bones would vanish; but before the perfume was near her nostrils, she recognized an ordinary myrrh to which a few drops of some ephemeral essence had been added. Vinodius ruffled her curls, and she tried to smile, as if the room were full of sunlight (which it was) and not this bleak and terrible anxiety. "I have been sitting patiently in the heat for hours, while Secunda dressed my hair. Must you destroy the girl's work in a minute?"

"The only use for pins is to take them out again," Vinodius teased. "What are we waiting for?" He pulled her down beside him on the couch, but as she slid into the familiar hollow of his arm, she knew that something had changed. Was it her own Secunda, with the apparently humble gestures? Or a girl on a farm? Nigridia . . . where had she heard that name; had her companion muttered it? She closed her eyes, and Vinodius whispered, "I did not come here to sleep." Her fear was changing to rage; it was not the ornaments that she would miss nor the out-of-season dishes, it was the roughness of his sword hand stroking her neck. The fool, she thought, suppose she had a few wrinkles from trying to dodge this strong Helvetian sun; what were they but a surface blemish easily hidden by paint? A farmer's daughter would squeal with fright if the governor touched her, and would be awed and clumsy; Secunda would refuse everything until her manumission was assured; but Vinodius was her life, she had even been faithful to him. She must sacrifice; somebody had bewitched him, she must hurry to the new soothsayer. Secunda! Nigridia! No, it was some other and terrible danger, and she clung to him as if they were home in that first tiny room at Genua. Secunda! Nigridia! What did those mere children know of love?

V

<hr>

VINODIUS stood for a moment, looking up at the sky. It had the slightly hollow surface of an over-polished shield. The official opening of the Games was just over, and now he would have to sit motionless in his seat for many hours. Sweat was pouring out of his body; however graceful the folds of a toga might be, it had been designed to guard a man from the sharp Roman winds, not to envelop him in what was almost African heat. In addition, he had on his official cloak, though in another moment or two he could let this slip from his arms. He noted with pleasure that there were no gaps between the spectators; they sat, shoulder to shoulder, up from the arena to the awning that stretched midway above the topmost tier. He raised his hand in salute to them, and there was a roar of joy.

Everybody relaxed as the governor sat down. Now that the ceremonies were finished, the place hummed with talk and wagers. The air was heavy with beast smells, sweat, leather, and the cheapest of cheap perfumes. Most people held a cloth soaked in these to their nostrils, from time to time, to deaden the smell of blood. There were occasional shrieks, the clatter of weapons, or a sudden burst of applause.

Vinodius let his gaze travel along the rows near him, and smiled. Dear Modestus, he thought, looking at an angular fellow three tiers away, so he had come to the Games to allay suspicion; but how miserable he was! He was holding a sweet-smelling shrub to his nose in such a manner that he could not see what was happening below him. Ah, Vinodius let his mantle slip from his shoulders into the hands of a slave, the man was a coward as well as a fool. Little did he suspect that with a wave of the hand, he might be writhing beneath them, at the side of the body of the escaped slave, about to drag to the barriers. If it had not been dangerous to interfere with the present precarious flow of oil to the population (Modestus had the biggest warehouse in Aventicum), he would have had the merchant arrested, because his name had headed the list of the so-called "peace party" that an informer had recently brought him; the conspirators wanted to negotiate with the tribes beyond the Rhine, an act that would cost the governor his post and the city its privileges, but the moment would come, it was only a question of waiting, and then the traitors would learn that though Rome could be merciful, to condone certain deeds was to spare the individual at the expense of the race.

It was a dangerous summer. Vinodius was not afraid of the barbarians. Raurica and Vindonissa were there to repulse them if they crossed the river in large numbers, but it was impossible to prevent a village or two from being burned, and then Modestus sent his agents to bring the survivors to the city where they tramped up and down, with a mixed and discontented rabble, yelling "We want peace." It was his duty to hold the province for the Empire. In two years, or perhaps three, Gallien would come with his legions, cross the Rhine, fight one battle, and the land would be secure again. It was merely a matter of patience and endurance, but the people thought only of their barns.

The Empire and I are one, Vinodius thought, wiping his hands on a wet cloth that his slave handed to him. He had not wanted to give up a third of his ever-dwindling fortune, to pay what seemed to be the worst lot of gladiators ever to step into an arena. Not that the peasants complained; they were shouting their heads off with joy. It would have been pleasant to have taken Tullia to the baths, and meet a couple of his fellow commanders again. Life in Aventicum had grown very lonely. There had been that villa in Lousonna, it would have been a cheaper place to live, and pleasant, after he retired; but he had known his duty, he had foregone them all, to give the Games. Already as the spectators bent forward, in a single continuous movement, their dangerous apathy broke; they were transferring their anger and unrest to the arena below them. Now they would have something to talk about on winter evenings: why a particular wager had been won or lost. Besides, he had been able to exact a heavy toll from Modestus and some of the citizens, and as a result, as another of his men had told him, they had had to dismiss several of their agents.

One fact was true. Something had happened to the world. He would have liked to flog the impudent youth who had said, loud enough too for him to hear, "With centuries in the shades, and only a few brief moments in the sun, I would rather lie in Phoebe's arms than watch two Thracians slashing each other." The boy had been the son of one of his friends, but it was ugly, as if a new dagger had been dropped and dented. He looked from face to face along the crowds; some were enthralled, some were anxious, others merely stared. They slouched forward with their elbows on their knees, they leaned back against the legs of the people behind them, but they were peasants, with hardly an elegant or handsome figure among them. Then his eyes fell gratefully upon a man whom he judged, even from this distance, to have been a soldier, because he was sitting upright and apparently explaining the swordplay to the boy beside him; yes, there was no school like the legion, Vinodius thought, his men were not plagued by some rhetorician's formulas.

"You won't find a better seat in the whole arena," Rufus boasted, "unless of course you are a young officer with more silver than sense to squander. This is the shady side, and we are looking directly at the centre, where they always place the principal combats." Nennius nodded, he was too excited to speak; he had never seen so vast a cluster of people before in his life, and all this had happened to him only because he had found an awl that Rufus had dropped, while collecting some harness to be mended, and had run after him with it to the leatherworker's booth.

"His time expired last year," Felix had explained afterwards, "but until they pay him his pension, if they ever do, Rufus will continue to make straps." There had been little for Nennius to do, so they had left him free to roam, and he had spent the previous days polishing tools, or blowing up the charcoal fire to heat the glue, and for reward, Rufus had told him stories about Pannonia. "All the men at Orba laugh at me when I say that I want to follow my father into the army," Nennius had confided to his new friend, "and I don't want myself to enter the garrison here. I should like to follow the Emperor himself."

Rufus had nodded gravely, and had taught the boy the ceremonial salute; then he had begged permission to take him to the Games. "A friend from the governor's bodyguard has given me two places," he had explained to Demetrius, "and the boy is so enthusiastic. It reminds me of my own youth."

A stout farmer near them mopped his forehead. There was an angry exclamation. Somebody, passing to his seat, had inadvertently kicked his neighbour. "Did you notice the governor's cloak?" the legionary asked. "You could almost call it purple, and it is worn only for the Games."

And the Guard! The men, in immense plumed helmets, stood motionless behind Vinodius. It was impossible to look at them for long; their polished breastplates reflected the sun like mirrors. "How hot it must be in that armour," Nennius continued in admiration; the glittering light made him feel slightly faint himself, and he had on only a thin tunic.

"It's a matter of training," Rufus answered carelessly, "but look, the gladiators are coming out. The real spectacle will begin with a battle between the Gauls and the Romans. It is excellent practice for you, watch how the masses move, because once you are in the ranks you will only see the comrades round you; but here, remember, the victory is arranged beforehand, it is a drill rather than a fight. Still, it is the way that the schools train their men. It gets their pupils used to the noises of the arena; and though they may get a cut or two, if one falls, his companions drag him away."

A number of slaves had planted freshly cut saplings in the ground, to represent the frontier. The Gauls crept forward between them, with long swords in their hands; and to mark the leader, one man wore an enamelled belt. First one group uttered a war cry, and then another, while the Romans locked their shields together and waited. They were fewer in number, but the more experienced men.

It had been good to watch the ceremonial again, Rufus thought, trying to see (but of course they were too far off) if the centurion behind Vinodius had on the baldric that he had made him. He supposed that it was talking to the boy, but his first campaign kept going round in his head, and particularly the night that he had stood beside a river, while his companions slept behind him, and the officer of the watch had come up to him on his rounds. "Do you know who you are?" the man had asked, and Rufus, who had just arrived from his preliminary training, had wondered whether he had lost his ears or understanding or both. "You are the rim of earth that is holding back the sea," the man had continued, sweeping his hand towards Pannonia. "Behind us are olives and corn, 'roads and peace,' as they teach us in the schools; but without you, sentry, and your companions, the Goths would snatch valley after valley, until the world that we value disappears. It does not matter what name the Emperor has, nor where his capital is. You matter, sentry, because you are keeping back the waves; the Empire is not the forum, nor the citizenship, but you." A strange fellow, too philosophical for a soldier, and strangers might have found such phrases treasonable, but they had all mourned when the man had been killed in a raid, a few weeks later, trying to drag a wounded man to safety.

"Oh!" Nennius leaned forward; he was ashamed to have let the cry escape his lips, because he was trying to imitate Rufus, and shout only after the main combats.

"There's a man down; is he killed, do you think? They're not dragging him out."

Rufus glanced down professionally, and shook his head. "It will end in a moment; nearly all the Gauls are down, or hidden among the bushes, which, incidentally, they ought to have watered; the leaves are withered already. No, it's a bad cut, but not mortal. Can you see the leech by the barrier? He is coming out to him now. I expect they will bandage him first, before they move him. Those young fellows are only half-schooled, but they are valuable. It costs nearly as much to train a first-class fighter as I shall get after twenty years' service."

"But I would rather be a soldier than a gladiator," Nennius protested.

"Of course, boy, a soldier is a citizen, but even if a gladiator was once free, and many of them are war captives, as you know, they never survive the schools. There is something about the training that dulls the senses; they have experience but no heart."

Rufus looked up at the governor again. The spectacle must be costing Vinodius a fortune, yet the citizens behind him, instead of being grateful, were grumbling at this very moment that he drank too much. Perhaps this was true, but the man had been a good soldier in his youth, and how could these fish dealers and shepherds understand what temptations a rich, provincial city offered after the austerity of a camp? "Try to spend your early service on the frontier," he said gravely to Nennius, "it's hard, it's cold, but . . ." he could not find the words and added, rather clumsily, "somehow you learn what is true. I hated coming here at first; a tribune had arranged my transfer with his own, because I had made him the chariot reins that had won him a race, but I became so restless after a month or two that I could have walked back to Pannonia. Then I married, the leather was good, and I finished out my service. Remember, once the legion sets its mark on you . . ." but for once he was talking to deaf ears. Nennius was not listening; the boy's eyes were fixed upon the two swordsmen who were now saluting the governor, while the crowd yelled. Rufus straightened himself in his chair, and sighed. In the lifting of the shield one of the two fellows reminded him of Festus, that impudent rascal who had more than once stolen his supper, who was always going to swim the Ister or capture a general, and who then had died, ingloriously, from an ague.

Vinodius watched the figures below him, with increasing irritation. They had cost him a thousand sesterces, and used their weapons less skilfully than his own bodyguard. His mouth was dry because it was forbidden to eat or drink at the Games, a survival, no doubt, from the days when human sacrifice was linked with single combat. But the wine that he had swallowed in great draughts before the ceremonies began had made him confused and sleepy. Both his shoulders prickled with

the heat and the appalling weight of even a thin toga,
but the real source of his annoyance was a rumour that
Thallus had repeated to him that morning. Statius, the
head of the gladiator school near Vindonissa, was match-
ing his best fighter against a young retiarus. Vinodius
had spent hours watching the men train; and though
the Thracian was good, he had been severely wounded
during the previous spring and he had a stiff shoulder.
Few would have noticed it (Vinodius smiled as he
thought of this), but after some minutes the man's guard
lowered a fraction, though otherwise he seemed as
speedy as ever. If the retiarus were inexperienced, with
merely a couple of local fights behind him, as the rival
trainer declared, it would not be important. Thallus had
heard, however, that the youth was an Iberian, with
several victories to his credit in the famous arenas of
southern Gaul. Vinodius had intended to bet on the
retiarus anyhow, and this was some salve to his conscience, but if what his steward said was true, many
spectators would lose their wagers. The swordsman was
the popular choice.

Vinodius held out his hand, and a slave behind him
gave him a damp cloth to cool his face. He ought to
warn his friends; then he remembered the farm that he
had wagered recklessly on the previous evening after a
cup too much of that wretchedly heavy Falernian. It
was the best one that he had left. The Greek's information might be false; the fellow hardly knew a sword
from its sheath, it was common knowledge that the

schools often arranged the winners beforehand among themselves, and anyhow, what could he do? Stop his own Games, acknowledge that he had left too many of the arrangements to inexperienced subordinates? "What can you prove?" Thallus had said. "The man has fought in Gaul, but never in Helvetia." Surely his friends knew enough to judge a man's chances for themselves? Leave it to the goddess of Fortune; and he murmured the usual prayer. All the same, no matter what thoughts came into his mind, the problem chafed him as roughly as a new, tight strap on the shoulder piece of a corselet.

"Clumsy fool!" There was a shrill scream, and a man toppled forward on to outstretched arms. Modestus turned a sallow green, and staggered towards the exit. "He won't get to the vomitorium in time," a tribune whispered, and the governor smiled. Still, it was so hot that it might be a touch of the sun; he had a headache himself, Vinodius reflected, he needed a change, to get back to the world. How tired he was of this provincial city, the resentful, frightened Helvetians, and boys who flattered him only because they wanted leave, or a transfer to the south. He had expected to be moved to Mediolanum himself, but though he had fought beside Gallien when the Emperor was a young man, with little hope of the purple, nobody had remembered to suggest his name when the new appointments were being made. It was time to act, unless he were content to linger sleepily here, and become a country landowner, once his term of service was over.

The first thing to do was to get rid of Tullia. She had lost her looks, and that Egyptian perfume she sprinkled on her hair made her grotesque rather than attractive. He would give her a little farm, if the retiarus won, on condition that she never saw him again. Then he must get his friends in Rome to find him some merchant's daughter, because gold was now more powerful than a name, and contrive to be called to the Emperor's camp. They said that Gallien was generous to those who had befriended him in his youth.

"But they've had no training at all!" Vinodius moistened his mouth with the tip of his tongue, as a gladiator below them lost his shield. "The people like it," his companion said soothingly, while a roar of laughter went up from the crowd. The heat seemed to grow, rather than lessen, with the shadows. He wiped his face once more, and decided that he would dismiss Thallus also, on his departure. He would never have tolerated such a creature in his house if it had not been so difficult to find an honest reckoner; and the Greek kept the warehouse tallies correct to the last, single grain. But he knew too much about plots and, for example, this retiarus. He must go, but only on the final day; how hilarious it would be to watch that solemn figure begging for mercy at his feet! Of course the man must have gold, he would have hidden it somewhere; what he would fear would be loss of protection. The fool had gambled everything upon his master's favour, and had enemies in every street.

The noises grew fainter, but his thirst increased. Had he told the centurion on duty to watch the gates? Modestus might try to smuggle out a messenger. He could not remember, and he did not want to send an order now and have them laughing in the guardhouse about his lapse of memory. There seemed to be a breeze, though it brought with it too heavy a scent of roses, and a quiet voice that said, "Excuse my tunic, but a toga is unsuitable for summer." It was Gallien; he was smiling at him, and looking hardly a year older than when they had fought beside each other on the frontier. He bowed and the voice continued, "Do you remember how my father sent us over the river together, with a single cloak, and only pulse for supper, as if cold and hunger were the only ways to leadership? You caught my roan for me once, when it ran away." The roses were making him drowsy, but he still heard himself answer, "That was in Gaul, and we were both young." "You are tired," Gallien continued, just as if he were still his soldier and not the Emperor. "I would not have left you in Aventicum so long, but the place was more important than it seemed. I can give you Narbonensis, or will you remain with me at my camp? It is lonely here," he looked down the row of rigid marble steps, "I need a friend." Then a messenger dashed into the courtyard, holding a tablet; men began to cheer, Vinodius blinked, there was no Emperor and no marble, but a tiny, blurred figure in the distance, looking up at him with uplifted sword. His companions glanced round to see why the governor did not give the signal for which the man was waiting; and as he held up his thumb, Vinodius realized guiltily that he had been fast asleep.

"How like Vinodius!" the young fellow next to them grumbled. "He gives us the Games, and then sends on rubbish like this." He yawned, and sniffed the myrrh-drenched cloth that he held between two fingers.

"But the next pair is excellent. I saw the Thracian last year myself, in Raurica."

"Oh, the retiarus always wins. I would rather watch two swordsmen."

It was the hottest moment of the day. Nennius had stared at the weapons so hard that his eyes were burning, as the two men came forward to salute. The one was a wiry fellow in a short, white tunic, handsome in a coarse way, with wrists as strong as a ballista. He wore no armour, but had a net draped over one shoulder, and a trident in his hand. "He's Iberian," Rufus remarked, "and they say he has only fought once before; that gives the other man an advantage. I wonder why they still cling to the trident; it's pure ornament, unless they use it for balance."

Men were shouting the odds, spectators who had dozed through the last fight were sitting upright in their seats again. "Have you ever seen them fight with the net?" the legionary asked, and Nennius shook his head.

"It is something you cannot teach a man," Rufus explained calmly. "Given time and patience any recruit can learn the elements of swordplay. But a net—to use it properly, a man has to have the feel of it in his body. It is tricky, and not straightforward; but watch how they will begin, the one quite still, the other all movement."

The two men took up their positions in the centre of the sand. They circled; the net swung, too short, and the Thracian cut at it, with a beautiful upward movement of the sword. Somehow the Iberian flicked the cords to safety and ran; all that they could see were his knees flashing, and the scuffle of dust. The Thracian swung back into defence, easily, with his back to the sun, and his shield well forward. He was far too experienced a fighter to tire himself out, chasing his opponent across the arena. "It's Etruscan," Vinodius whispered to the tribune beside him. "I saw such a figure once painted on the walls of a tomb." The artist had indicated the weight of the weapons, not by making them large, but by a flowing line of muscles underneath the straps of the greaves. He had been a boy when he had seen the painting, but he could recall the luck-bringing lizard that had disappeared between two stones as if it were in front of him now; but had he, or had he not, warned that boy at the guardhouse to check all strangers? Vinodius yawned; perhaps it was unimportant after all. The Iberian prowled forward, with a leopard-like crouch, his black, curly hair stuck out from the tight fillet like a mane. He stopped, retreated a few steps, then moved forward, coming always in a series of rushes and leaps, first from one side, then from the other, waiting, swinging the gathered net, throwing it over his shoulder, as any fisherman might do for sport, by a pool near the rocks.

"The man's no novice," Rufus said. The big amphitheatre grew gradually still. Nennius fixed his gaze upon the shadows in the sand (his own heart was beating too fast), upon the great, rigid plume and the shadowy, pulsating cords.

Thallus was right—Vinodius gripped the marble edges of his seat—this retiarus was worthy to fight in Rome; he knew every trick, he must have been in a dozen arenas. The net shot out again, not slowly, as when one was tossed from a ship and it sank gradually beneath the surface of the water, but as a hunter might fling one to catch a lion in its leap. "Ha!" the crowd yelled as if they had a single throat; the Thracian sprang as if his corselet were made of shell. "He's down," they gasped. "No!" The Iberian had sprung away; he darted towards the barriers, to turn suddenly, and gather up the partially destroyed net. "Missed by a finger's length," Rufus said excitedly, "but the Thracian almost caught him."

Vinodius felt that his throat would burst. The swordsman was winning, and he had risked his best farm upon the chance turn of a wrist! The figures flickered to and fro, like dancing spots when a man caught full sunlight in his eyes. "Grant us a full life and a swift death," he murmured; it might be only an old army proverb, but it was true. He had let things drift; yet now, just as he had made up his mind to act, his future was balanced on a sword edge, because if the retiarus lost, he would have to borrow, yes, even from Modestus, to pay his debts. If he could have one swallow of wine, less than the dregs in a cup, his head would clear. "Hit him!" There was another roar, the crowd's sympathy was with the Thracian whom many of the soldiers had seen at Raurica; the man stepped sideways, and the Iberian only saved himself from overbalancing by sticking his trident into the earth.

"Watch!" Rufus shouted; he gripped the boy's arm so hard that Nennius almost screamed. "He caught him with one of the weights," the legionary growled. They saw the Thracian's point drop forward. He recovered himself; the Iberian turned, as if for another run back, suddenly his arm went up, he did not throw, the swords-man stabbed at the air, there was a leap, a shout, the net fell almost gently over its victim. Men rose yelling in their seats, the Iberian jerked the cords tight, and looked up, his hand on the handle of his dagger.

Vinodius gave the signal for mercy, but it was too late; somehow as the trap had caught him, the Thracian's sword had twisted under him, and he had been driven downwards on to the edge of his own blade.

"You are not at the Games?"

The trader was dozing on a bench under the trees,

and opened his eyes reluctantly to see Gallio standing in front of him. "No, I had a touch of fever this morning." Actually he had seldom felt so well, but it was one of his principles never to attack established custom; so if his customers delighted in the arena, he pretended to agree with them. The fever was simply an excellent excuse to cover his day at the inn. People would be sympathetic in the evening, the losers would tell him that the goddess Fortuna had protected him, and the winners might buy a trifle out of sympathy. "The weather . . ." he said, with a vague movement of the hand, "but it is passing."

"Shall I disturb you if I sit here a few moments?"

On many occasions Demetrius would have replied with a blunt yes, but he had been alone all day, and was beginning to tire of his own company. "You are welcome; but if you would tell my man, he is sleeping in the yard, to find us a little wine, it may aid our conversation. I expect the kitchen is empty."

Gallio raced off joyfully, and the trader sat up and stretched himself. Even at this distance, he could hear the roars of the crowd; it was all very well to say that most of the men were criminals, and that death was swifter and more merciful in the amphitheatre than in prison. Justice frequently depended on protection and bribes; he had had one or two narrow escapes himself, and besides, if some wretched fellow were tormented till he ran away, the man showed spirit, and deserved to be employed rather than slaughtered. It was a waste of valuable material. He yawned; there was a particularly violent yell, followed by absolute silence. One of the big combats had ended, no doubt, and they were dragging out the bodies. "I told them to mix the wine with three cups of water," Gallio said, coming back and sitting down on a low stool in front of him, "I thought with fever you would want it weak."

Demetrius nodded gravely in thanks. "There is this advantage about the Games, the flies have abandoned us for the arena."

"It is barbarous," Gallio looked up angrily; "if the men must die, why not give them hemlock?"

Demetrius nodded; he did not want to be drawn into any discussion of the subject, and at that moment a decrepit slave (certainly the oldest that the inn possessed) hobbled out with the wine and two cups. It was a general holiday, and those who were not at the amphitheatre had gone bathing in the near-by lake.

"I knew you understood, when I came over the other evening," Gallio said, after they had made the customary libation and had drunk to each other. "You are a traveller, and can imagine what it is like to be tethered all the year round in this provincial backwater."

The trader might have no knowledge of painting, but he understood youth.

"When I was your age, my father kept telling me that I should drown in a shipwreck. I wanted to go to the Indus."

"And did you?" Gallio asked eagerly.

"No, my father died when I was still quite young, so I had to take over the mules. It costs a lot to keep them in fodder; and then dreams are dangerous."

"But you know the world! The innkeeper here told me that you were no ordinary merchant, going up and down the same road every year."

"I have been to many places, yes, and at your age it is natural to be restless." They drank to each other again, and Demetrius smiled. It was not true to say that he had become a sober merchant over night. There had been a ruinous expedition into Gaul, when he had saved his animals and himself through pure luck.

"I cannot learn more here, and I want to study. I want to go to Rome."

"But it costs many sesterces to live in a city," the trader objected doubtfully; "few men buy paintings."

"But they buy these." Gallio handed him a small painted box with three divisions for a woman's ointments inside it. The trader took it with a pang of disappointment; so this was just a new approach to selling him some goods. And he was about to begin the bargain by remarking that the shape was no longer fashionable, when the boy reassured him unexpectedly. "I do not want you to buy it, I brought it for your opinion. Could I sell these in Rome?"

"I thought that you were going to paint the governor's wall?"

"Thallus does not like me; he will not ask him. I suppose it is because I am married."

"Life would be hard in Rome, unless you had a patron."

"They say that the Emperor favours artists, and because of his example, many senators are redecorating their villas. He has his own walls hung with fresh rose leaves every evening."

"And he is a soldier!" Demetrius groaned.

"And a good one," Gallio said confidently, "I know some swordplay myself." He held out his arm for inspection, with the very gesture of a legionary. "I was always in fights," he grinned, as the trader felt his muscles with approbation. "My father came from Gaul, so the boys in my street called me a foreigner. First I used my fists, afterwards I had some lessons with the sword."

Demetrius considered the youth again. He was as out of place in this stolid country town as a chariot horse linked to a team of oxen. He turned the box round, opened it once more, and ran his thumb over the partitions. "It depends, I think, upon the strength of your will. If you can keep to your craft, and not waste time, running round the market place to look at the Scythians, yes, you might survive. But it's partly the material; you won't find this wood further south."

"But I turn here like a beast in a cage," the boy pleaded. "I know my last work is not good. Look at this," he thrust a smaller box into the trader's hands, "there is no expression in the faces. My tools reflect what I feel. Even my father, before he died last year, told me to go to another city. I am willing to pay; take me with you when you leave."

"And your wife?" Demetrius asked.

"She will go with me. How many pieces would you ask?" He took a little bag that was too thin to contain many coins out of his tunic.

"By Hercules, it was a trick, the Thracian was a far better man." A farmer stumbled into the courtyard, already half drunk. He had stayed at the inn on the previous night. "The other man was hardly more than a dancer," he snarled, "and I wagered the price of three lambs. . . ." He sat down so heavily on the bench that the trader's wine would have gone over if Demetrius had not saved it with a deft snatch. "They set a trap, and all of us fell into it. But I'd like to know what they would do for their banquets, unless we grew their corn for them."

"Have some wine," Demetrius suggested, holding out a hastily filled cup. The man took it, drained it, and held it out to be refilled. "It's time there was a change," he grunted, looking about him with bloodshot eyes. "I shouldn't care if the Alemanni did cross the Rhine. They couldn't be worse than our present rulers."

Drunk or sober, twenty years ago the man would have been arrested for such words, but now there were so many emperors, in the East, in Gaul, in Rome, it was hard to remember their names. Demetrius looked at the shadows; they were lengthening under the tree, and vendors were beginning to cry their wares again. There were other voices outside, people were beginning to drift home.

"The Thracian was a soldier, and they let him be killed by a worm." The farmer banged his fist down on his knees; he looked around as if he wanted to pick a quarrel. "Your Vinodius took half the winnings," he said, glaring at Gallio; "he bet on the dancer."

Demetrius caught Gallio's eye, and they stood up together. "Afraid?" the farmer jeered; but the merchant answered quietly, "I am only going to get some more Rhaetian, I shall be back in a moment." It was going to be a disagreeable evening, full of quarrels. "Is there nowhere in this town," he whispered to Gallio, "where a man can be quiet?"

"Come with me." They walked briskly through the crowd, in the opposite direction from the amphitheatre, towards the outskirts of the town. Most of the spectators had stopped in the wine shops, but plenty of people who had lost their wagers, like the farmer, were shouting at each other in the streets. "It wasn't a fight, it was murder." There was the sound of a blow, and several onlookers tried to pull two youths apart, who were smashing at each other with their fists. "It's the fighting; it has gone to their heads," Gallio said disdainfully, "but we shall reach a quiet path in a moment. I am taking you to my house." Vinodius had won his bets. He would probably buy the fur cloak. Demetrius glanced at the eager figure in front of him, and decided that he could afford to be generous. There was a steady sale for boxes in the cities, and a little help now might mean good business in the future. The boy would walk some of his restlessness away, crossing the Alps. "Gallio," he panted, "it is uphill, and I had a fever this morning"; and, as the painter turned to wait for him, he continued, "A friend of mine is going in three days to Mediolanum. A silversmith and his family are joining him, and I think you should accompany them. It will be better for your wife to travel with other women. I will speak to him about the price."

"A silversmith! That must be Uppius. He told me that he was waiting until next year."

"But he cannot sell his wares. The farmers are frightened of invasion. He is going to join his brother at Mediolanum while he still has enough to pay the journey. From there, you can easily go to Rome next spring."

The leaves were dusty in the little gardens, but the gay, green apples on a small tree were beginning to turn gold. There was a noise of bees. "It's peaceful here," Demetrius said, wiping his forehead, "are you sure you want to leave?"

"It's not my country," Gallio answered, kicking a pebble into the rank summer grass.

"If I help you to get a mule, can you be ready in three days?"

"I am ready now," Gallio said simply, as they stopped in front of a wooden fence. A girl was filling a jar of water at the fountain. She smiled at them, as Gallio unfastened the gate. "Sabina," he shouted gaily, "we have a guest." She came toward them so shyly that Demetrius could hardly hear the habitual words of welcome, and he looked up sorrowfully at the painter. How could he transplant a mountain child like this to the narrow, airless rooms of a Roman house?

Demetrius walked slowly down the temple steps at peace with the world. A number of traders were leaving together after the Games, and they had all offered a joint sacrifice of two fine lambs to Hermes. Demetrius did not care for a man to be too religious; it usually meant that he was either intolerant or had a twisted character; but he believed in correct behaviour and in making the proper sacrifice at the beginning and end of a journey. The gods, he supposed, were like the emperors, and could mete out good and evil as they chose; only, unlike the emperors, they were eternal. Hermes was the patron of traders; he forgave them the shifts to which they were driven, showed them the way, and helped them as strangers. "Bless my journey home," Demetrius prayed, as they had all prayed together in the sanctuary, before he stepped solemnly on to the road.

It was still early, but it had been hot in front of the altar, listening to the innumerable prayers. The auguries had not been altogether favourable, but their voyage would be blessed if they departed at once; every sign urged swiftness. The old rogue, Demetrius thought; dozens of peasants went to the temple, and the priest had probably heard that snow was to be expected earlier than usual. It was astonishing how these Helvetians knew, almost to an hour, when the wind would change or there was risk of a drought.

It was a pleasant town. Demetrius paused to look at the Treasury inside its stone wall, and the villas scattered within shady gardens. Yet each year they were a little more neglected; the temple yard had not been properly swept, a latch was hanging loose from a shutter, the gutter was choked by a dirty mass of what had once been somebody's garland. He wondered why the place had changed so much during the six years since his first visit. Then there had been chariots on the streets, and many wagons, an indefinable sense of the city being alive. Was the Empire too big? Yet it had been larger, and nobody had counted the provinces. Were the young so ungrateful? It seemed to him that there was just the same proportion of honest men and rogues as in his childhood. There was the constant talk about invasion; nobody now was certain as to who was emperor of what, but the Treasury still functioned reasonably well, most roads got mended, trade went on, yet he could not deny the change. Something had happened; it was as if a sentry had been asked to keep one watch too many, and his fibre had snapped. Even the weather was out of tune with the seasons, and it was as hot in this valley as on the lava blocks in Sicily. If he did not have a drink, after all those hymns, he would roll over like a sun-struck mule, leaving Felix with his woeful prophecies fulfilled to the letter, to lead the party to Verona.

Everybody knew Demetrius, and he was hailed from all sides as he came up to the assembly point in the middle of the square. The poorer people had left; they would drink their last toasts outside the city, where the taverns were cheaper, as there was no toll to pay on the wine, but the merchants themselves were sitting on stools and benches, over a light meal. The first day's march was a short one, and they would wait for the dust to subside before following their mules. Where was Gallio, he wondered. This was a scene for a painter; all crafts were represented in the crowd, there were farmers who wanted to travel as far as they could in company, donkeys laden with jars of honey packed in straw, for which Aventicum was famous, some smart legionaries in summer tunics, and townspeople come to make a last minute sale, to say farewell to friends, or merely out of curiosity. "Have a drink with me," a dark-skinned little Syrian shouted, and he made a place for the trader to sit beside him.

It was Kallistus, the man whose party Gallio had joined. "You heard the auguries," he said anxiously to Demetrius. "Are you not coming with us?"

"In a few days. I shall join you at Lousonna."

"What a season! Everybody wants to sell you something, but they are all unwilling to buy anything in return."

"It's the worst summer I have known, but the honey is good. I tasted the new crop the other evening."

"It's too dry with us," Kallistus said; "there is something in the mountain honey that makes it last longer. It is one of the few things that I can still be sure of selling. I am glad that you brought me that broad-shouldered fellow who wants to go to Mediolanum. Did you hear that a farmer was murdered yesterday just outside the town? Poor fellow, he only had a few pieces he had won at the Games; if he had drunk them away he would still be alive."

"Oh!" Demetrius started. He had dreamed the previous night that a horde of galloping horses were kicking down the walls of the inn. It was naturally the dreadful meal that the innkeeper had served them, and it did a man no good to let himself be swayed by fancies. Still, the soothsayers declared that such a dream could be a warning of disaster. He felt suddenly so uneasy that he was tempted to call Felix, and order him to harness the mules; then he remembered the fur cloak, and shook his head.

"I wish we had more soldiers on the roads, instead of so many sentries here. Six years ago, the road to Lousonna was as safe as this street."

"You still have business at Aventicum?" Kallistus looked at him so suspiciously that Demetrius, with a glance to see that his neighbours were not listening, said in a low whisper, "It's my shoulder; the leech has promised me that if I follow his treatment for another few days, he can restore the use of it. You know what gossip is! If I tell it to anyone but yourself, it will be rumoured that I am disabled, and that ruffian at the inn will double the price of his miserable fodder." Actually the wound had healed, but he did not want even his friend to know that it was possible that the governor would summon him.

"Gossip is the curse of affairs," Kallistus said, with a nod of comprehension. "Your secret is safe with me; but even at the cost of some stiffness, do not wait too long. The snows come suddenly after violent summers."

The stool was hard, and his neighbour's knees were pressing uncomfortably against his back; yet in spite of this, and used as he was to similar scenes, Demetrius watched the square with a fascination that increased, rather than decreased, with age. How he would miss it all when he was settled at Verona! Small groups plodded by, their packs on their shoulders, the itinerant followers of the Games. Their patched coats were as colorful as a mosaic in this sunlight. A boy in a yellow tunic, with a rust-brown cloak rolled over his shoulder, bobbed up and down as he balanced himself on a wall until the jerking colours almost made him look like an apple. There was a flute player in a green cap, next to a peasant in such tattered garments that he might have twisted them together out of reeds, but they laughed and joked, although the gods knew that they had little to rejoice about, as they drifted from village to village, wherever there was a feast or local procession. They had not even the security of the slaves, their weapons were a ready tongue and a witty answer; presently the cold would drive them to winter quarters, an old barn or some stable at Lousonna, but people liked their gaiety, and permitted them a license denied to the stolid citizen, with his craft, food, and a roof.

"Today, the small vendor is more successful than I am," Kallistus grumbled. "Do you see that man?" He pointed to a short, broad-shouldered fellow who was tying a pan and a poker together, while his wife stood beside him, with an empty brazier on her head. "He is taking home four pieces of silver, all gained by selling pancakes at a penny apiece. Of course it was a country audience."

"If it had not been for that attack at Saltus I should have been half-way to the Alps. I have never known trade as bad as this summer."

A child acrobat pushed his palm under their noses, while his master folded up the mat that had been used for his performance. The boy's body was well formed, and would have been handsome if it had been less dusty, but behind his smile there was the cunning of a miserly peasant, and his eyes never left their hands. "I've seen better tumblers; but here, take this," Kallistus said, "it may save you a beating." Demetrius added a coin, and felt the hard pad of a small animal close over his fingers. The boy ran back to his owner; they both bowed, and walked briskly away down the square, followed by a melancholy flute player. "I saw the rogue slip one of our coins into his cheek," Kallistus laughed, "but it is a hard life, made up of dust and slaps."

"Come back!" A fellow roared from the middle of a small crowd advancing towards them. "By Hercules, once I shake the dust of this town from my sandals, I never want to hear of it again." There was a long scar from ear to chin across the man's face.

"It's Statius," Kallistus whispered, "he owned the Thracian."

"Why did you match your man against the retiarus?" a young officer enquired. "A man in heavy armor has no chance against them."

"No chance! I've knocked out a couple of them myself in my time," Status sneered, "but you have to be swift, to attack the first minute before you tire, or your opponent can measure the distance. In my last fight, we knew that the winner was to be given his liberty, the tribunes put their silver on the man with the net, but I was the one to be freed."

An admirer came up with a goblet of wine, but Statius pushed it aside, and continued angrily, "The Thracian was worth ten thousand sesterces."

"Hardly ten thousand," another officer called from the edge of the crowd.

"It was what he won last year at Raurica."

"You matched him too soon, after such a cut on the shoulder."

"It had healed. No, it was a swindle, a trap. They said that the other fellow was a novice. A novice! Yes, he had seen so many arenas that he must have been reborn, to be able to count them again on his fingers."

"Have a drink and part friends," the first officer begged.

Statius took the cup, but stood with the white and terrifying scar disfiguring his face, without making a libation. "We know we are doomed," he grumbled. "Of the men who entered the school with me, I was the only one to win my freedom. Yet there is a way of dying, even on the sand. After I have trained a man for month after month, I like to see him have a chance."

"Take this with you for the journey," another admirer said, coming up with a small wine skin, "your luck will turn next year."

"Half of you do not know what fighting is. We spend months teaching a man to hold his shield correctly, and then you shout that it's too slow. All you want is a rush and a stab, as if we were beasts. Are you ready?" He swung angrily round, and brought the short stick he carried smartly down on the slave that stood behind him. "No, if you want to see my men fight again, you will have to come to Italy."

"If you find a new man," the second officer laughed, "you will forgive us by the spring." The group moved off; several of the men had bandaged heads or arms, and one, flushed with fever, sat with a disabled leg on a large mule. A slave carried a dented shield and several broken swords, the grim and only memorial to the losers. There was a smell of grass, and the faint scent of a creeper that had grown up one of the pillars of the inn. Several offered them food, but Statius shook his head. He strode off angrily, with hardly a farewell, followed by a dozen little boys who were trying anxiously to keep in step with the gladiators.

"Statius is honest in his way," Kallistus said, "more honest than the men who make money out of these contests. I heard that he wept all evening over the Thracian, less because of the loss than because the man was his friend."

"It's a brutal business," the trader muttered.

"Like life."

A shepherd stopped, his crook over his shoulder, searching the line of people for a friend. "Till next summer," he shouted when he saw him, "lambs and ewes, ewes and lambs, I shall hear nothing but bleats and the buzzing of flies till I have counted ten moons on my fingers, and the fair comes round again. I would almost as soon be a soldier."

"You wouldn't, not after the first day," a legionary grunted.

"Here come the mules," Kallistus said, "where is the innkeeper? I must pay for our wine. After these stories about attacks and murders, we are travelling together in one large band."

Demetrius strolled over towards Sabina. She was standing beside a small donkey, and he noticed that she had been crying. "Gallio will be here in a moment," she said, "he had some trouble with his mule."

Demetrius grinned. "It takes a few years to establish confidence with the animals. I started when I was twelve." Sabina's eyes started to fill with tears again, and he hastened to reassure her. "The men who are taking you down are good fellows, they will help you."

"I shall never see my village again."

"Perhaps you will. I did not want to encourage your husband, because nobody leaves his birthplace lightly for a foreign city. But his work is good. You need have no fear. He can sell all the boxes he can paint at Mediolanum. Keep him to boxes, though; there is not enough money today for painted walls."

"Did he tell you," Sabina asked suddenly, as if she were compelled to confide in somebody, "that he took me without a dowry?"

"No, he only said that he was fortunate to have you for a wife."

Sabina managed to smile. "Gallio had brought his father up to the mountains, because he thought that the air would be better during summer. I wish you could have seen him. Gallio painted him once as Nestor; there was something regal about the old man, and ancient like the stories. He was not as simple as the people here. I used to bring them goat's milk every evening; then one night a kid escaped, and Gallio helped me look for it. Afterwards he wanted to paint me and then, it still seems like a dream, when it was time for them to return to the city, his father spoke to my uncle, because my parents were dead, and we were married."

"It will be easier once you start," the trader said gently.

"You saw our home; I was so happy here. I only missed the mountain air a little, but Gallio was always restless."

"It's his age, but he has talent. I think you will like the south, especially if he can find you some rooms with a little garden."

"But do the ladies at Mediolanum wear their hair like the wives of the officials here? It must take them half a day to arrange those curls. I am just a country girl; Gallio will leave me."

He probably will, Demetrius thought; he was sorry for the child, being torn from everything that she knew, and from any relatives that she might have (and how these hill villages stuck together!), but he said encouragingly, "No, the fashions are simpler in the south. The styles here are those of twenty years ago. Whenever you miss your mountains," he added, "look in your mirror; your eyes are the blue of the bells growing up the slopes."

Sabina tried to smile, and Gallio came up eagerly. "I thought both packs were equally balanced," he laughed, "but the mule knew otherwise."

"You can't trick them even once," Demetrius said, scratching his ear. He was pleased with himself because he had persuaded Kallistus to take the couple with him for only three pieces. It was partly due to Gallio's shoulders and his knowledge of swordplay, and Sabina had

133

promised to help the other merchant's wife. Then he had negotiated the sale of a mule; it had a rubbed patch and was a bad-tempered beast, but that was due to the stupidity of its former owner; it would double in value after it had been in good hands for a month. In return, Gallio had promised to come to Verona the next spring before he went on to Rome, and bring him some boxes. These, Demetrius knew, he could sell very profitably if there was no expense of transportation. "No regrets at leaving?" he asked.

"None, I feel I am born again; I shall be grateful to you as long as I live."

"It's harder for your wife, she is leaving her home."

"But you want to go," Gallio looked at Sabina in surprise, as if it had never occurred to him that she might be unhappy at leaving. "You never once asked me to take you back to your village. Oh, when you see the temples in Rome, you will forget these stark Helvetian mountains."

"Girls and children, Gallio, have their roots where they were grown. Give her a garden; she wants grass, not paint.

"But you are a fool to leave!" a friend came up to Gallio, "there will be no hunting round Rome, and I've heard their water is bad."

"I shall miss our sword bouts together," Gallio laughed, "but life is not only made up of trapping hares. Besides, you ought to come with us. Once your uncle returns, you will never be allowed outside the forum. Plinius is to be a lawyer," he explained.

"I do not want to leave Aventicum. I was born here. I like the sound of what you call our barbarous dialect, and I want to go on swimming in our own lake."

"Ready?" Kallistus asked, coming up to where they stood. A man slapped the first mule with his stick, and the group started forward. "If you are ever in trouble, come to me at Verona," Demetrius said, as Gallio tugged at the halter of his beast. "No, let the animal have his head, he will follow the others." Sabina rode off, after the other women; she did not look round. The trader was careful with his coins, but on an impulse he slipped something into the overseer's hand. "Look after the girl," he whispered, "it is hard to leave one's native town."

The man winked. "With a pretty child like that," he whispered, "all the men will look after her."

"See you in Lousonna," Kallistus shouted. He followed with two other merchants, a little behind the others.

Demetrius waved, then he went slowly back to his place again; within a few moments the square had emptied itself, and he was now the only stranger left at the inn. He was glad he had no roots, as Sabina had, to make him sorrowful. Aventicum was pleasant enough, with the distant sound of water and the faint scents of the first plums falling on to the grass, but he would miss the splash of the anchors, or the clatter of the children

135

carrying fish up to the market, if he had to spend his life here. He looked down at his feet that had trodden so many miles of ground, and felt them long for the soft grass of a cool path in the mountains. "Wandering," he whispered to himself, "if it's in the blood, you feel it till the Messenger calls for you." Yet he pitied Sabina, leaving the country she loved a little further behind her every day, and he was uneasy because he knew that he should have added the kid he vowed to offer, after the attack at Saltus, to the general sacrifice. Money was short, and it would be easier to buy it after he had returned to Verona. He sighed; the truth of the matter was, he was hungry. He clapped his hands, and when a slave ran up to him, in spite of the extravagance ordered himself a fresh mountain trout and some of the sun-dried meat for which the region was famous.

VI

THE storm would not break, and the evening was going to be hotter than the day. The heat was likely to endure until the grape harvest; and now that the Games were over, people were listless and irritable. It would have been wiser to wait another few days, Demetrius knew, before presenting himself at the governor's villa. The costs of the arena were probably revolving in the man's head, as often and as dangerously as the net of the retiarus, but the trader felt so uneasy that he had sent a messenger to Thallus, begging him to arrange an early interview. He told himself a dozen times an hour that this was the natural result of the attack above Saltus; but as soon as he woke up in the morning, or if he felt a twinge of pain in his shoulder, he seemed to hear a voice in his head saying, "Get to the pass, get to the pass," although it would be a full two months until the snows.

It was only pride that kept him at Aventicum. The dust spoke to him, as he was fond of saying; and ever since his father had died, leaving him the mules and a small sum of money, he had returned with a profit to Verona every season. He wanted to close this last summer with a gain; oh, not a spectacular one, like the time when they had saved a Roman official from thieves and the man had given them five hundred sesterces, but with a few coins in his hand, and the knowledge that he had been successful up to his final journey.

There was one advantage about this late, hot afternoon—the streets were deserted. Demetrius walked slowly in front of his two men, who were panting less from the weight of the bales than from the want of air, but he did not need the bird that rose from a courtyard on his left hand to warn him that the day was inauspicious. He dreaded the interview, but he had told himself so often that Vinodius was going to buy the fur-lined cloak, that he firmly believed he could depart only after he had made the sale. "We must be prepared for difficulties, Felix," he said slowly.

The man shifted the bale strap and grunted. They were walking now beside the long wall that divided the governor's garden from the street. "They say he has no money," Felix said finally, "he sold land, and a number of slaves to pay for the Games."

"It would be a pity to have to carry the cloak back to Verona, though we might get a better price for it there."

Felix had been with his master too many years to reply. He knew that the trader was merely thinking aloud. A dove called to its mate, otherwise there was no sound, everybody on the other side of the wall was still asleep.

"May Hermes protect us! How suddenly we remember things." Demetrius stopped to look up at the branch of a cherry tree that hung over the road. "It was an afternoon like this, but earlier, in May, when I lost myself, gathering fruit. That was before you came to us, Felix; it was on my first journey, before I was twelve years old. We were walking along a valley, and it was so hot that I could hardly put one foot in front of the other, when I saw a cherry tree in an abandoned field. I slipped away without my father seeing me go; and it wasn't stealing either, because the grass had not been cut, and there wasn't a roof for miles. There was so much fruit that after I had eaten my fill, and had picked a hat full to take to my father, I had only stripped a couple of the lower boughs. The cherries looked so gay swinging above me, and the meadow was more full of scents than a country temple is of spices at a festival, so there I sat in the shade, and I suppose I went to sleep. Anyhow, when I woke it was almost nightfall, and I could not see a sign of the mules. I can tell you I was frightened."

"It is never safe to leave the road," Felix answered gravely.

"I ran. How I ran! I was sure that I was lost. As the shadows lengthened, I expected a bandit to spring out on me with a dagger, and then I came to a fork in the road. I didn't know which way to turn, yet I was afraid

139

to stop where I was. I shut my eyes and prayed to Hermes, and at that moment I saw my father and two of his men coming back on their mules. They had not missed me until they halted."

"It was lucky for you that you stopped at the cross roads."

"Yes; how my father beat me when I came up to them! But I did not mind the pain, I was so happy to be found again."

"We always feel the lashes. I wonder if they are easier to bear if we know we have deserved them?"

"Your religion would do away with the whip," Demetrius said, looking at the servant curiously.

"We say that if men follow the laws of God, there is no need for it."

Very impractical, Demetrius thought; but the essential rule in trading was never to anger another man's gods, and Felix was the best servant that he had. He wondered if it were true that the Empress belonged to what had been called "the slave's religion" in his youth? The eastern rituals had a great attraction for women. "My father often whipped me, but it did me good," Demetrius continued; "aie, what a headstrong boy I was when I was young."

Still, I wriggled my way out of as many beatings as I got, the trader thought, and remembering these early days his apprehensions lessened, while in this shady road the sun seemed less fierce.

The gate of the villa was open, and the doorkeeper

was sitting in the shade. "I was bidden to present myself this evening," Demetrius said, bowing humbly, and pressing a coin into the man's hand. He noticed that the two steps leading up from the street had not been swept, but were still covered with the day's dust; so it must be true that Vinodius had sold some of his slaves.

"You are wasting your time. If my master had wanted anything, he would have sent for you on your arrival."

Demetrius bowed again and said quietly, "I was summoned here by the governor's steward."

"A likely story," the man grunted; because of the heat he had on only a short and rumpled tunic; "they would have told me, if you had been expected."

The trader looked down at the man's sandals, and the long white scar on the fellow's sunburnt leg. Yes, the saying was true; it was neither the dangers of the road nor the tolls of the customhouse that counted, the real skill in trading was how to get past the doorkeeper. He could motion you to a place in the cool courtyard, or deny you admittance at will. With a part of his mind, Demetrius almost longed to be turned away; he felt too weary to beg and flatter on this torrid evening, but there was his pride, the cunning that his fellows said would get him "past Cerberus," and he repeated only, "Sir, I am obeying my orders."

"And I, mine." The man stretched his staff insolently in front of the open gate.

The air was suffocating. The merchant felt that he could no longer breathe. Why, it was almost as if he were a boy again, with the two fellows whom he had followed so trustingly forcing a bandage into his mouth that stank of oil and sour wine. Here was another omen, because that early and dreadful experience of his life only came back to him in times of danger. How he had gasped and struggled, and when he had come to his senses in the open air with a gash in his tongue that had not healed for a week, his father had thrashed him in front of all the men as if he had been a runaway. Yet, if his father's servant had not seen him trotting after the two sailors (why, one of them had had a scar like this doorkeeper had, across his leg, and that was, no doubt, why he now remembered the scene so vividly) he would have wakened up the next day in the hold of the Syrian slave ship with a collar round his neck, and his life wrecked, owing to a moment of boyish disobedience. He could still feel the bandage; he was choking, his heart was beating; he even put his finger on his throat to be sure that there was no strap binding him, and then they both heard a rustle of sandals, and as the door-keeper turned, Demetrius caught sight of the burn of a whip lash across the fellow's shoulder. "Punctual, I see, but sellers, alone among us, have a sense of time," and Thallus, in thin and newly washed linen, came towards them.

"It is thanks to you that I shall not be late. We look too tattered, it seems, after our summer on the road, to be admitted."

"I had no orders," the doorkeeper complained, looking at the bales with a scowl. He knew that he had lost a second piece of silver.

Thallus made no reply, but led the way into a long courtyard. It had once been a garden, but now nothing was alive in it, except for a few ancient trees. He sat down on a bench under the terrace and motioned Demetrius to take a place beside him. "Tell your men to spread out the furs."

"Oh, forgive me, sir," (it was essential to remain on formal terms while in the Governor's house), "we are humble people, who have had to learn our lessons on the soles of our feet. The governor will prefer to see the cloak taken out of the bale. He might suspect, otherwise, that it had been offered to every tribune at Vindonissa."

"Therefore you have the sacks resealed at every halt," Thallus said, with a laugh.

Demetrius shrugged his shoulders. "Sir, we all have to live." He looked up at Thallus, and added almost in a whisper, "I would not have sent the messenger to you, but we are meeting at Lousonna this year, and travelling together for safety. There is much unrest on the roads."

"I was waiting for a fortunate moment. At first, my master was busy getting the city cleared up after the Games. Then that woman of his was ill, although in my opinion he is better tempered when he does not see her. He graciously gave me a new tunic."

"A tunic! When may I see it? You will allow me to entertain you before I leave."

143

"Actually the money was for wine; but wine, alas, belongs to the gods who know how to use it. They absorb the aroma, and leave the liquid in its goblet." Thallus pressed the palm of his hand against his stomach, in the by now familiar gesture, as if the mere idea had given him a twinge of pain.

"I have a powder against disorders of the bowels," Demetrius said quickly, but as if it were an observation without importance. "At Mediolanum, I was in agony for a week, till a friend brought me the mixture and cured me. He was a Greek; for all our faults," and the merchant smiled, "we have some knowledge of herbs."

"Yes, we had a good physician here, but he took fright this spring at some fable in the market place, and went down to Rome."

"My powder would save you the cost of a physician. It should be taken at sunset. I fear with a little wine."

"Has it to be taken often?" Thallus could not keep the eagerness out of his eyes, and Demetrius knew that his friend would now do all he could to smooth the way towards a sale. Every man had his price, but it was often difficult to guess what it might be, upon the flash of a moment.

"No, only when you need it. Felix, get me those phials," the trader walked over to his servants who were standing beside the bales, just inside the doorway. "I have a second and more powerful remedy, but I left this at my lodging; it is for use in moments of extreme urgency, and is worth its weight in gold."

"It is strange," Thallus said meditatively, "I cannot understand why these pains plague me. I have been so frugal in my habits."

"I noticed that when we met," Demetrius bowed, "you follow the philosophers. It is the only road to happiness."

"Is it?" Thallus sighed. "My master eats half a lamb and washes it down with nine bowls of Rhaetian, and then flings himself on his couch and sleeps like a baby. As for myself, the nights I spend in agony . . ." Thallus spread out his hands in a gesture of desolation. "Yet I seldom touch anything but water."

"It is often harder to find good water than good wine, but try my powder. I remember how I suffered at Mediolanum. They say I kept screaming for the Messenger to come and put me out of my pain."

"I prefer the light of day to the shades," Thallus remonstrated unphilosophically, "but tell me, and speak the truth for once, is your drug better than spurge?"

"Cover as much as will go on a knife point with wine, and try it this evening," Demetrius suggested, taking a straw-wrapped bottle from his servant. "I brought some with me to use myself, but if a friend is sick . . ." He held the phial out to Thallus, who snatched it greedily.

"And the price?"

"Take silver from you! And for an act of mercy! Never!" Demetrius threw up his hands. "I will send you the other drug tonight. It is said to be a Cretan herb."

"If all the plants supposed to come from that island

really grew there, Crete would stretch to the Pillars of Hercules."

"I know, I know," the trader shrugged his shoulders, "a physician's herbs usually come from his own yard. But in this case, a friend gave it to me, and not for money either, an unusual act among merchants."

Thallus nodded. "We will see, we will see. You are sure that the powder contains no hellebore; I do not want to vomit."

"I am a merchant, not a juggler," Demetrius answered, with some indignation.

"Well, I will try the remedy tonight. And now, wait. I think I hear footsteps. The governor often walks in the garden before dining. Be sure that the cloak is the one that you showed me. We had a lot of trouble about that Thracian who was killed, and he is still irritable."

Demetrius got up and stood in front of the bales, ready to prostrate himself humbly as soon as Vinodius entered the courtyard. The Romans sneered at such eastern salutations, but they liked them; and once, when he had omitted it, an official had had him chased out of the house with whip and dogs, upon some pretext that he had been impudent. His hands were trembling, and he guessed from the movements of his servant's lips that Felix was praying. The calculations that usually soothed him when waiting for a client would not stay in his head; the profit of his journey depended upon the price that he could get for the furs, yet he knew in his heart that he did not wish to sell the garment to the governor. What he wanted to do was to keep the pelts himself! The idea startled him so much that he swore softly, and Felix looked up in surprise. And a fine sight he would look, he thought, with the bottom hanging over his arm, like a woman's robe, because it was too long, while he marched up and down his cabbage rows! No, it was meant for an officer, but was Vinodius the right man? He would throw it down, and forget it on an angle of the wall, or fling it round him after he came in, white with dust, from the parade ground. Well, it was too late now. It was a pity that the commander was not Valerius; Valerius would have looked magnificent in such a cloak, and would have known how to care for it.

"Furs! On a day like this! The man's a fool, but then all traders are crazy."

Demetrius had just time to notice before he prostrated himself, that Vinodius looked much less heavy in a tunic than his toga, but he was not young, and his cheeks had begun to sag.

"My steward tells me that you have also got amber," Vinodius continued; "you may show it to me, although you could not have come at a worse moment. The treasury is empty."

"It was rumoured in the market place that my lord was lucky with his wagers," Demetrius said softly, as he got to his feet.

"Lucky! Praise be to Fortune that she was with me,

147

but naturally I bet on the retiarus; the other fellow had a stiff left arm."

Demetrius would have liked to reply that not all men were Roman or trained to weapons; instead he said quietly, as he unwrapped a strip of soft leather, "I can have this set in any way you wish."

"What is it? A pebble?" the Roman joked, although just as aware as the trader that no finer piece of amber had come to Aventicum for years. Points of light flickered across the base, and as he held it up, it changed into a sea, the colour of the setting sun.

"It is good amber," Demetrius said simply.

"A mere pebble," Vinodius repeated.

"If you prefer the larger kind, I have them," the trader replied, untying the strings of a second and bigger bag. Of course, he was tired of wandering; by Hermes, if he got home this time safely, he would never venture forth again, but as he looked at the stones gleaming on his palm, he remembered a river captain telling him at the bartering place that the gems came from sands where the north wind rose, and girls danced throughout a night that was brighter than day. The man himself had used the word goddess, but the trader distrusted fables, and suspected that divers found them in a mine under the sea. All agreed that they were then passed from hand to hand, a year's journey down the rivers, until they reached the south. He had also heard another story. Up in the north, there were men who spoke a second language, and held strange ceremonies,

148

with singing and a fire, that the tribes on either side of them were unable to understand. Could these be Greek wanderers, and his heart began to beat, some colony from the time of the migrations, defending the customs of the golden age? What he might learn if he could reach that shore! When spring came round, and his fellows took to the roads, how could he bear standing still in a field while he tied up vine shoots with unskilled fingers?

"The amber comes from the dancing ground of the muses," he said to Vinodius, "the grains that stick to it are not real sand, but dust from spiced woods."

Vinodius turned the second brooch over in his hand; it had been set in northern pattern by a Greek freedman attached to the garrison at Vindonissa. "It would look well on a winter cloak," Demetrius ventured, "and remind you of sunshine when the snows are on the ground."

"A winter cloak. My steward said something about a pelt you had, that might do for hunting. Show it to me; but by Hercules, if it is not a good piece, out you go with your bales."

Unlike Thallus, the man had been drinking already, Demetrius decided, for his face was full of tiny, swollen veins. "It's a cape that the governor of Vindonissa wanted to buy, but I did not show it to him; it is too good for a frontier town."

Felix bent over the bag; the trader noticed that he started, but the fellow said nothing as he handed him the cloak. Then Demetrius saw to his horror that in place of the furs for which, having given weapons for them, he had risked imprisonment and flogging, he had in his hand an ordinary centurion's cape. He could not blame his men, because he had packed the bale himself, and had left, no doubt, the real garment at the inn. He felt a wave of fear go to the bottom of his spine. "Fur is scarce," he muttered hurriedly, "and mortals may do what they please, but winter comes again." He did not spread the cloak, but moved it this way and that, while sweat, only it came from terror rather than heat, ran down his cheeks and over the palms of his hands. He would sacrifice another kid to Hermes if he got back to the inn without a beating.

"That thing!" Vinodius said contemptuously—fortunately he was too hot to examine it closely—"take it away, it makes me pant to look at it. And I have all the furs I want. But I might take a brooch . . . what other pieces have you got?"

"Pack the fur up," Demetrius said, in almost audible relief, as he took another packet from the wallet at his own belt. He always kept the best things on his own person; it impressed buyers more, they imagined then that he was selling something that he had meant to keep for himself. "You won't see this every day," he said proudly, "not even in Rome."

Vinodius turned the brooch over in his hand and held it up to the light. Even if a traveller exaggerated his adventures, Demetrius thought, it was foolish not to listen to him. The chance remark of a sailor had led a friend of his to fortune. The man had followed a clue to some city in the East, and had returned with a bag of ancient coins, inscribed with Greek names. Oh, if he were a young man he would try the venture to the frozen seas. Each tribe wanted to keep its trade to itself, but sometimes it was a question of language. Once you could persuade the barbarians that you were neither a Roman nor a settler, but just a man seeking for a temple or his ancestor, they were often friendly and helpful. "It comes from the land of the Hyperboreans," he added, in the flowery language expected from traders, but amber knew the secret ways and paths; oh, why was it the only colour and silence?

"It's amber, I won't say more than that," Vinodius remarked, rubbing it on his tunic; "well, what do you want for it?"

Demetrius hesitated a second; he must not name a sum that was either too high or too low. "It would be a gift at a hundred sesterces," he suggested, but nobody heard him. There was a noise at the gate, Thallus went forward with an indignant face, Vinodius looked up angrily, then a centurion burst into the atrium, shouting in the purest Roman Latin, "Out of the way, I tell you, I *must* see him." It was a man from the first cohort at Lousonna. Sweat was running down his face; but with dust over his clothes, and his legs a mass of bramble scratches, he looked little different from one of his own soldiers. "They're here," he panted, hardly making the gesture of a salute, "get the men to the defences."

"Here! Who are here? The Alemanni?"

"Raurica has fallen."

"Raurica! Impossible."

The man shrugged his shoulders helplessly. "I was on leave at Balma, recovering from a fever, when the first survivors poured in yesterday. I thought it was a raid, till a man came from one of the mountain outposts; his comrades had been overwhelmed, and he had seen the smoke from the burning city. The tribes have crossed the Rhine, and there is no barrier left between their armies and us."

Vinodius looked coolly and with almost a trace of anger at the messenger. "It is a raid, a larger one than usual, but I shall need more proof that Raurica is lost than the cries of a few Helvetians. They always panic when their villages are burned. You had a fever, you said?"

"It is over now, I was to return to my post at Lousonna tomorrow."

"Even if the tribes have broken through, they will soon have the cohorts from Vindonissa on their flanks. There are times when we see everything a little larger than it actually is, and I will not allow the population to panic because a few frontier posts have been overrun. We will order a double guard to be set as a precaution. Wash away the dust and get fresh clothes, then you can tell me your story while we dine this evening. As for you," Vinodius glanced round at Demetrius who had tried to force himself behind a pillar, "one syllable about what you have heard and it will be hanging, not flogging, remember. Look to them, Thallus."

There was silence until Vinodius had left the atrium; then the centurion broke into a hoarse whisper. "Raurica *has fallen*, they swarmed across the river one dark night, it was worse than an avalanche; there may be captives, but there are no survivors."

"How long have we got?" Demetrius often wondered afterwards at his impudence, but perhaps it was his almost insolent questioning of the officer that had saved them.

"The tribes are better disciplined than they were, and will advance rapidly, hoping to surprise us. We ought to withdraw the outposts, the best soldiers we have are on the hills." Demetrius nodded; for the flash of a second he saw Domina Julia coming towards him along the terrace with her salves; then the centurion continued, "He thinks I am a fever-stricken fool, but it's true, I tell you. Raurica has fallen. How can I make him believe me?"

"Leave it to the townspeople once fugitives arrive. And Vindonissa? Can that garrison help us?"

The man shrugged his shoulders again. "What can they do? They have got to hold their part of the river."

"Go to the inn and pack, Felix," the trader whispered, "they shut the gates at sunset. But you heard what the governor said? One word, and we shall be arrested and tortured." He looked up at Thallus, but the fellow had turned green, and there was the same sickly smell hanging about his now-creased tunic that criminals had when they were dragged from their cages and driven into the arena. "You would like a bath?" Demetrius asked, as if he were an under-steward of the household, and nudged Thallus; "please call for a slave."

Thallus clapped his hands. An African came running up and Thallus managed to gasp, "Take the officer to the guest chamber." Demetrius noticed that the veins at the back of the man's legs were twitching as he followed the slave towards the other side of the house; then the two Greeks looked at one another.

"The only chance you have is to come with us," Demetrius said quietly.

"And my possessions?" Even in his terror, Thallus looked at the engraved cornelian ring that he wore on his left hand.

"Do you think you can stand a siege?" Demetrius continued implacably; "you cannot even bear the sights in the arena. There will be no water, and many, many arrows." The steward's contemptuous words during their last meeting still rang in his ears, "You traders only see the dust on which you tread, not the larger issues of the Empire."

"They will not dare to attack Aventicum."

"Raurica was garrisoned by the best soldiers that we had; and you heard what the officer said, there are no survivors. You can no more stop the Alemanni now than you can hold a river in flood."

"We shall be murdered on the roads," Thallus almost screamed.

The trader was silent, he had seen fugitives in panic. Oh, why had he come here instead of going directly to Pennilocus? It was his pride, his false and foolish pride that had destroyed him.

"Aie! Why should I have to suffer for the faults of others? I have prayed, I have fasted. . . ." Thallus struck his head with the palm of his hand.

And the gods might have been better pleased, Demetrius thought, if you had helped your fellow-men. Aie. He must hurry himself, they would close the gates in less than an hour, and by the morning nobody would be allowed to leave the city. Why had he deluded himself that the rescue at Saltus had been a fortunate augury?

Then he remembered Valerius, and the feeling of security that they had had, inside Orba. "You can save us both if you want, Thallus, but if we are to escape, I need your help, and that swiftly."

"Escape?" Thallus looked up with a gleam of hope in his eyes.

"As the officer has just said, Vinodius will forget the outposts. If we can send word to Valerius to withdraw from Orba, his men will guard us as far as Pennilocus. Get me a tablet and your master's seal."

"How dare I ask my master for a military order?"

"Get the seal," Demetrius said impatiently, "if you want to save your life. Have you ever felt an arrow point? It stings," and instinctively he rubbed his stiff shoulder.

"Suppose I get away," Thallus wailed, "how am I to live? What prospects are there for me?"

"Prospects! There are plenty of opportunities in Verona for a man with your experience. Besides, we are both Greeks; you can remain with me until you find another master. Only now there is not a moment to lose. You told me that the governor does not require you in the evening, so he will not notice your absence. You said, as well, that you write his commands out for him. Get a tablet at once. It is only the seal that is important."

Thallus was twisting the folds of his tunic into shreds with his fingers. The paving stone at his feet was discoloured by the petals that had fallen from a half-dead, white rose tree in an earthenware jar beside them. The sky above the centre of the atrium, that had been a merciless blue since dawn, was beginning to wither into tiny, yellow rifts. "I must go," Demetrius said, "and take my chance alone; but as a last favour, Thallus, see me past that doorkeeper. I shall come to Cerberus soon enough, without meeting him here."

Thallus seemed to spring to life as Demetrius moved. "The tally," he shouted, "I had it for the grain sack this morning. It is not quite the same as the military seal, but if I am careful, I doubt if they will notice. Wait for me here."

"No," the trader shook his head. "I must collect my men. We shall wait for you as long as we dare, at the gate. Don't overload yourself with more than you can carry," he added, "unless you can find a mule."

156

"Hurry!" It was Thallus now who moved as if he could not be still. Demetrius could hardly keep up with the man's long legs; the secretary darted forward as if he were a suddenly disturbed crane. Yet as soon as they came to the steps, where the doorkeeper eyed them disdainfully from his stool, he was as calm and aloof as if a long old age at Aventicum stretched tranquilly before him. "I will acquaint you with my master's decision about the cloak tomorrow," he said curtly; "meantime farewell, and do not come here again until we summon you."

The men followed the mules down the road. They had left Demetrius arguing with the innkeeper over the final payments. "It's a good thing that we packed the bales this morning," Felix said, "but I felt in my bones that once Alexander (this was their private name for Demetrius) had seen the governor, he would want to leave."

Unless Thallus arrived within the next five minutes, they would have to risk the journey alone. A man marched out, carrying a basket covered with leaves; the owners of the little stalls along the road were putting away their unsold goods till morning. It was not only Aventicum but the commerce of a province that was ending. In spite of what he had said once to Valerius, the Alemanni pillaged but they did not settle. He wished that he could go up to these people and whisper, "Raurica has fallen," but they would merely laugh at him, and the soldiers would arrest him. If Vinodius were wise, he would evacuate the city, and withdraw with every man whom he could muster to the passes. The area was too large, and his troops too few, for a successful defence.

"*Everything moves.*" Demetrius looked up at the peeling walls in front of him, and murmured the unfashionable tenet. Everybody laughed at Heracleitus today. Yet the wind stirred, the rain and the ocean had their beat, the earth was never still; unless there were freedom of movement between road and road, country and country, even from craft to craft and mystery to mystery, something like death happened. People stared at the narrow limits in front of them, until they neither saw nor heard the rumours on their own border. Then the barbarians moved, in a brutal, continuous wave; but what riches, and what beauty, vanished in the tumult!

"He might have waited till tomorrow," one of the men grumbled.

"Why? The wine is cheaper outside and just as good." One of the men, a cheerful little African, prodded the beasts back into line, out of the path of some loitering citizens.

"Even you will need a drink tonight," the first fellow said with a grin, "it must have been a hot walk with that heavy sack, and do you know what was inside it?" He leaned over and pretended to whisper into the mule's ear. "Harsh words and no coins." They all laughed.

"Oh, we sold a bit of amber," Felix said indifferently, though all the pieces were in the bag at his side. "We did not sell the cloak, but it was a bad moment after the Games." The men had suspected something on his return, and he wanted them to believe that their hasty departure was due to the threat of extra tolls, or a fine. They must not know the truth until they were well out of the city. The news had not surprised him, he had been expecting it himself all summer. People would not listen to the warning of God; he thought of the impious spectacle in the arena, and shivered. They would not work, they would not pray, grown men lay on couches, singing foolish songs, they tossed their slaves from one household to the other at pleasure. The bitter years of his childhood rose in his throat. In spite of the priest at Verona (who had argued and prayed with him for half a night) he could not suppress a feeling of exhilaration that another city was about to fall, that hundreds more Romans would soon know the kicks, curses, cold and hunger that had been his own portion, or that worst experience of all: having to kneel at an owner's whim, to receive a beating meant for somebody else. "There is strength in forgiveness," the priest had told him; and because the Christians had promised him equality, he had agreed. Yet he could feel no pity for Aventicum, doomed though he knew it to be; let them wail till they envied the comrades who had died, till they gave up hope. Yes, the Christians could tell him what they liked; it was not a sin to want to die.

"Keep to your side of the road." A shopkeeper shook his fist angrily at one of the mules. The animal had almost bumped into a man who was selecting a gaily painted toy for his child. Useless stuff, Felix grunted to himself, as the man turned the wheels of the little wooden chariot, with a work-stained finger. They would toss such things for firewood under the cauldrons of boiling oil, unless the tribes surprised the city before resistance could be organized. He had once picked up such an object himself, a broken, three-legged horse that a Roman child had dropped into a patch of weeds. "You cannot expect a boy of five to be a man," he had shouted at the priest throughout that long evening, when they were arguing about baptism. "They beat me, they beat me, not for stealing, nobody wanted the thing, but for touching a toy that had belonged to a Roman. I hate them . . ." he had screamed on, only submitting at the finish because he had been unable to endure the slow, quiet prayers a moment longer. No, nothing could wash such memories from his mind, nothing could give him peace. "But it was the world you wanted," the soft, maddening voice had continued, "you longed to be a legionary, and carry the eagles yourself." He had let the old man talk, he was used to concealing his feelings, but he had gone to the Christians for equality, not doctrine. "Wearing a hat will make no difference," he had heard that sentence fifty times, whenever he had brought his money for safekeeping to the church, "freedom is in the heart." The fools, let them chatter; they had no knowledge of the market place, what could they feel of it, they had been born free. He was aware that people disliked him, that his comrades called him surly Felix; but because he had never once given them a glass of wine, nor allowed himself a single indulgence, with the help of Demetrius, and after twenty years of counting pennies like a miser, he had been solemnly freed at the last winter festival; and the instant that he had set the cap of liberty on his head, it was as if his five senses had been restored to him. It was circumstances, and not the Mysteries, that made a man.

Otherwise his life had hardly changed. Demetrius had driven a hard bargain, and he would have to serve the trader until he had paid off the part of the manumission fees that he had borrowed from him. He was also a sinner in the eyes of the Church (did they but know!) because he had let his master represent him as old, and almost worthless, so that the tax might be lower. The State, that men so worshipped, knew how to exact its gold. A man could not even free some old woman who had been his foster mother, without paying a portion of her value to the Treasury. And then the priest talked about forgiveness! He slapped at a fly that had just settled on a mule's hindquarter, and shouted angrily, "Unless you hurry, the gates will be shut."

"Master Felix, keep an eye on the boy; he doesn't want to go home."

Felix looked up, startled, to see Rufus standing in front of him, holding Nennius by the belt. The boy looked sulky, and had a small bundle under his arm. "He tells me that you are leaving tonight; is it the heat, or rumours of war, that are driving you away so soon?"

He stared at the harness maker for a moment without speaking. Here was a man who could mend straps more skilfully than any craftsman north of Verona; yet in spite of this, and of his service, he was still waiting for half of the miserable pension due to him. Vinodius had had enough for the Games! Men who had sweated their lives out on the hard roads died in poverty.

"The boy came, begging me to take him in. I would gladly teach him all I know, but I must have his guardian's consent."

"How can I go back to Orba?" Nennius grumbled sulkily. "Domina Julia does not like me. I love this city, and I can join my legion here."

A man's concern was to look after himself. Pity was a woman's toy, though he had never noticed that they were particularly merciful; yet if Rufus had not warned them about that landslide the previous year, they might have taken the short cut and got caught in a second avalanche. Then he would have died before he had had the right to wear a hat on his head.

"Has the governor ordered you away?" Rufus asked anxiously. "I could let you have some straps if you need them, and you can pay for them next year."

"A moment," Felix said; the mules were already far

up the road. "Join the others at once, Nennius, you promised to be obedient. You cannot stay here without permission." Something in his voice made the boy turn, and mutter a farewell; then he trotted off sullenly, with tears of disappointment in his eyes. The two men stared at each other again. Felix opened his mouth, but the warning would not come. If the harness maker betrayed them, they would certainly be tortured.

"Something has happened! Have they arrested Master Demetrius?" The legionary wiped his forehead with the back of his hand.

"You warned us about the landslide last year but . . . ," that sound could not be his voice, Felix thought, it sounded as if he were being suffocated. "My life is in your hands. Can I trust you to be silent?"

"The Alemanni!" Rufus said gravely, and Felix nodded.

"Raurica has fallen," he whispered, with a glance to be sure that no passers-by heard him, "there are no survivors."

"Raurica!" Rufus stared at him, as if he had been struck by the moon.

"An officer came from the outposts, as we were selling the governor a cloak."

"Raurica! But they had half a legion!" Rufus shook his head, as if the freedman must be demented. Felix shrugged his shoulders. Life was sin, and evil and misery; what did it matter if the legionary betrayed them? "They surprised the city, and there are thousands of them, marching upon Aventicum. Get your arms, and come with us. Pennilocus is the first place we can hold."

Rufus looked down the road. "I believe you," he said, "though there is nobody else in this place whom I would believe, not even your master; though I suppose, as traders go, he is honest. But you are right, until the news is proclaimed I am free to choose; and since my wife died, I have no roots here. Only I shall return to Valerius; I served under him once, at Orba."

"My master told me that the outposts west of Aventicum have been ordered to fall back to Lousonna. There would be no time for them to reach the city. We expect to join up with the Orba men ourselves at the crossroads. Come with us, only do not tell Demetrius that I warned you."

"By Hercules, you have saved my life, and I will not say a word," Rufus slapped his great fist down on the freedman's shoulder so vigorously that Felix jumped. "I am surprised Vinodius had the sense to remember the outposts. I must get my tools, without them I am a beggar, but I shall catch you up on the road, if not at the gate." He turned off towards his booth that was not twenty yards away, with the same steady stride that had carried him over leagues of the Empire. Felix felt his heart beating with excitement; peril makes men brothers, he thought grimly, but he had spoken as one free man to another. Then he noticed that the mules were almost out of sight, and forgetting all dignity, he started to run after them.

There was an orange haze along the western horizon, and the light was lessening with surprising speed. Officially the gate was shut at sunset, but on these summer evenings it was often open until an hour or two afterwards. Revellers walked to the cheaper wine houses outside the city boundary, under the pretext that it was cooler to sleep in the country; or farmers went to an inn a mile away, so that they could begin their journey home at dawn. It was too hot to travel once the sun was up. The more austere citizens grumbled about the laxity of the guards, but tonight a few moments might tip the scales between ruin and safety. Once the news spread, the roads would be jammed with peasants and cattle; they might save their lives if they abandoned the mules, but in this event they would starve at Lousonna, without the means to continue their journey. They dared not take to the less known tracks across the hills without an escort. Everything depended upon Nennius being able to take the orders to Valerius in time; the minutes were passing one by one, and there were no signs of the steward.

Would Thallus never come? Demetrius shifted from one leg to another; both ached, not from standing but with nerves. He was not only anxious but uncomfortable; there were a number of coins in the wallet at his belt, and there had not been time to change into his travelling clothes. He had these, and the special cloak that he had forgotten to take to Vinodius, in a bundle under his arm. Two men passed, already half drunk, croaking rather than singing a harvest song. The merchant sighed over the silver that he had had to pay at the inn, money that would be lost in the flames, or looted by the barbarians. He had not even had time to bargain properly, so the rascal there had grossly overcharged him. The innkeeper had supposed, in common with his men, that the governor had ordered him to leave, and was prepared to take full advantage of his haste.

The trader looked up the street. "Hurry, Thallus," he muttered, as if his friend could hear him. The road was empty now, except for two or three men waiting to pass the guards. One of them greeted him, and to his astonishment it was the harness mender, Rufus; he had a sack over his shoulder, and a couple of tools swinging from a broad, new belt. "I have got a job to do on a farm," the man whispered, because he was not supposed to work except in the city, "may I follow your men as far as the crossroads; it is lonely marching alone."

Demetrius nodded. "You will find Felix at the second tavern, the one beside three poplar trees, but we shall start before dawn. If there is any truth in the old saying that a red sky means settled weather, it will be even hotter tomorrow than it has been today."

The legionary muttered thanks, and turned towards the guards with a joke. They knew him and waved him through, without his having to unfasten the sack. He plodded up the road that was crackling with grasshoppers, and the trader felt more cheerful; he liked Rufus, and might be able to warn him once they were in the country, provided that he could catch him when Felix was out of earshot. He had hoped that Felix might have lost some of his surliness after his manumission, but the man had not changed. He hated the world and everything that was in it.

There was a clatter of steps, and the soldiers straightened themselves, as if they expected an officer. "Quickly, we must go," Demetrius said to the one servant he had kept with him when he had sent the others with the mules to wait outside the town. A small coin freed them from having to open their bundles, and once they were outside the gate, he looked back for the last time. There, hurrying towards them, was a man in an enormous travelling cloak, followed by a tiny boy leading a gigantic mule. Was it, it could not be, yes, it was, Thallus! "Hurry," Demetrius shouted; the guards were beginning to push the gates forward. "A moment," Thallus yelled, holding up his hand; he was now within hailing distance. The officer looked up to see why his men had stopped; suddenly he began to laugh, there was something irresistibly comic about the group, they came up pompously as if they were straight out of one of the new satires. "A moment," Thallus repeated, panting a little, "I have work to do outside this evening."

"Work!" Everybody began to laugh. "With Ercole,

no doubt." He kept the most notorious tavern in the neighbourhood. A sentry barred the way; it was too late, Demetrius thought, they had lost by a single moment. Suddenly he heard his friend singing, a coin was tossed into the air, the soldiers bent double with laughter. Then the officer recognized Thallus, and muttered, "It's the secretary of the governor." He winked, and waved to the extraordinary group to pass through the already half-closed gates. "It's all right this evening," he admonished, "but another time try to be a little earlier. When there are rumours of the Alemanni around," and he laughed, "our friends the citizens get frightened if I do not lock them safely into their cages before nightfall."

Felix walked desperately back and forth in front of the inn. The mules were bedded down, the men were asleep. He would like to join them himself; the march the next day would be long and arduous and it might be hours before they could rest again. Where was Demetrius? Why had he not come? Had his master's love of a bargain trapped him in that doomed place? Peace is a gift only of the grave, he repeated, shrugging his shoulders, happiness is an illusion; but suddenly his philosophy cracked. He trembled as he thought of the spears and the shouts; he wanted to run across the plain and down the valley; he even longed to see that old stable again at Verona, where he had spent so many angry hours during the winter days, mending sacks and sorting bales.

Suppose the governor had sent for them after all, fearing some leakage of the news? His knees twitched, sweat ran down his back. Perhaps they had seized Demetrius, and were searching now for the rest of the party? There was always the lure of some small, incidental plunder for the soldiers, even if their officer sealed up the merchandise. He sat down on a stone; everywhere was dark, but the path was just visible in the starlight. Ought he to wake the men, abandon the animals, and start for the lake? No, such a move would arouse the innkeeper's suspicions. The man would think that they had killed their master. How could six men hide—they would be as easy to find as hares on cropped fields. The darkness seemed to fill with whispers urging him to go forward alone; wasn't he a freedman now, what did he owe to Demetrius, or the Romans? If the soldiers found him, it might mean slavery again, and that thought was worse than torture. He knew the way, he was still swift of foot; was there any reason why he should not strike across the hills towards Lousonna, instead of struggling with a lot of lazy mules, or waiting until escape was impossible? He was kind to me when I had that fever, Felix thought, he trusted me with his goods; some blurred phrase about fidelity sung in his head, he could not remember the words, but only the old priest's voice. *I want to go, I ought to stay*. Felix shuddered because he had seen men branded. *I want to go*. He got up, and stared at the blackness. Then (like the glad, triumphant sound of a trumpet before the Games) he heard a voice that he knew. Demetrius was coming up the road, but he had people with him, and an immense and unfamiliar mule.

"I was afraid that you had been caught inside Aventicum," Felix said, going to meet them.

"We almost were. I got across myself, but Master Thallus, you remember Master Thallus," and Felix bowed, "nearly got jammed between the gate and the wall."

"They said that I was late." An unrecognizable voice came from under a peasant's broad-brimmed hat. "I had to use the poor authority I then possessed with the centurion."

"You made some most unphilosophical statements," Demetrius chuckled.

"For once, the sins of my youth were useful."

"He sang," Demetrius said with huge delight, "a wine song and a love song mixed up together. Then he tottered towards the officer—a centurion and of the Guard —tossed him a silver penny, and bade him drink to Bacchus. Such impudence! How the soldiers laughed. I suspect, Thallus, that you were an actor in your youth. Why did you tell me that you walked the gardens of the philosophers? And then, oh then," the trader shook with merriment, "the mule got jammed between the gates."

"I have not had your experience in loading it," Thallus said stiffly; the bag that he was carrying at his girdle puffed the cloak up, until he looked more like a lop-sided dovecot than a man, "but we are here."

Oh, those Greeks! Risk or no risk, how they clung to each other, Felix thought, as he took his master's bundle.

"Don't look so anxious, Felix; Master Thallus has brought something with him that will take us safely to Pennilocus. Here is a command to the garrison at Orba, to escort us there."

"I wrote," Thallus murmured with some pride, "that we are carrying the archives."

"How do we know that Orba has not been overrun already?" The light-hearted banter of the Greeks had angered him, and Felix wished that there had been light enough to see the fear that his question must bring to their eyes.

"I do not think that the Alemanni have reached the hills," Thallus answered unexpectedly. "If I know anything of the tribes, all will have wanted to take part in the looting of Raurica. We have a day, but no longer."

"Everything is ready, I got a small sack of extra meal and the wine, as you ordered; we can start as soon as it is light."

"And the boy?" Thallus asked.

"Yes, Nennius. Can we trust him, do you think, to carry the tablet to Orba, or shall we send another of the men with him?"

"No," Felix shook his head, "he will be safer alone; they will think he is a herd boy returning to his farm.

I will wake him earlier and tell him what has happened, as soon as we can see the road. He ought to reach Orba by nightfall."

They stood there silently for a moment, while the scent of some newly cut grass doubled its intensity in the cool evening air. He was alive, Felix thought, for once without bitterness; he would always remember how the hay smelt, it was more delicate than beans. The mule moved sleepily towards the yard, dragging Aristo rather than being led by him. They could hear men snoring, and the trader yawned. "Come with me, Thallus," he whispered, "we must get all the sleep we can. There is a long march in front of us tomorrow."

VII

Orba.

THEY had come to the crossroads. The men were
sitting with their feet in a small stream, next to a
tumble-down barn, about a quarter of a mile along the
track up to Orba. They had piled their bales under the
wall, and hobbled the mules. A peasant had left his field
to hear the news, and then had sold them food and wine
for twice their value, together with the promise that his
wife and himself might accompany them to Lousonna.
Even if they had not agreed to wait here for Valerius,
they could have gone no further. They had been on the
march since before dawn.

Demetrius stretched himself; as he went over the
events of this extraordinary day in his mind, it was pleasant to feel cool water slipping between his toes. Nennius
had been the first to leave, but it had been almost cold,
and the sky had been bird-coloured, something that was
neither grey nor dusky nor white, when they had stumbled sleepily out from the courtyard. At first they had
made good progress, passing only a few farmers on their

way home from market; then, before they had been travelling an hour, Thallus had insisted upon stopping in front of a stable, to bargain coldly with a countryman for a rough but docile pony. His judgment had been correct, the trader thought, looking across at his friend who was lying on the ground, wrapped up in a huge cloak. He was too unused to travel to be able to make this forced journey on foot.

They had stopped for a brief rest towards midday; and, under the pretext of testing the weight of a bale, Demetrius had whispered the news to the legionary. Rufus had been profuse in protesting his gratitude, but the trader had had an uneasy feeling that the man had heard already about Raurica. "Don't tell Felix," he had whispered, "he has a strange fear of disobeying a command, and they threatened us with torture if we spoke of it." Then they had grinned together like conspirators.

It had been a little later, at noon, when the alarm had reached them. At one moment they had been lying on a bank, eating a crust of bread with some really excellent goat's-milk cheese, and everything had been perfectly still. Then, as if the grasses had been flattened (though if he had looked at them carefully, he would have seen, of course, that they were still upright), men had rushed on to the roads with sheep, with carts, with women holding baskets on their heads, with crying children stumbling over dogs. "The Alemanni," a farmer had shouted to them. "Run, they are coming!" But as far as the horizon there was nothing but stubble, a few apple

trees, and here and there a roof. There was neither
smoke nor sign of war; only if a girl were fearful, she
might have imagined that the shadowy trees on the
neighbouring hills were full of the gathering tribes, and
the grinding of wheels on the small, slithering stones
was the sound of them, sharpening arrows. "We have
one day," Thallus had said once more in dry, precise
tones, as if he were measuring the salvage of some crop.
"Yes, but we must move," the trader had answered,
helping the men himself to load the tired and irritated
mules; "in a few hours the roads will be impassable."

They had made fair progress for another five miles;
then they had had to crawl along at a caterpillar's pace
until they had reached the appointed meeting place.
They could rest here, if not for the night, at least until
there was word from Valerius.

"How long will it be before the garrison arrives?" It
was the tenth time that Thallus had asked the question,
the only trace of anxiety that he had shown, Demetrius
thought, as he looked up at his friend.

"Nennius can take footpaths that are not wide enough
for mules. He should be at Orba by sunset. They can
evacuate the place quickly, and it is about two hours
away, or a little longer, at night."

"I shall try to get some sleep," Thallus answered
mournfully; he was rubbing his chafed legs with some
salve.

Demetrius nodded. It was a peaceful landscape. A
tiny breeze had sprung up, but only the top leaves

moved. They were near an apple tree, and the trader expected that the weight of the fruit would anchor the boughs, but the movement caught them, and they swayed gently to and fro. The wife of the old labourer came towards them with more bread, and the wind, except that it was too gentle to be called by such a name, rumpled the fringe of her yellow scarf. In the fading light, the wild flowers and the stubble were the same pale straw colour. It was quiet, quiet . . . yet at this very moment, Aventicum might be burning. He tried to think of the trees that he had watched so often during the last weeks, and of Sabina's garden. He knew what happened when a city was sacked, but for the moment all he could remember was tranquillity and shade.

The trader folded up his cloak to spread underneath him, but he was too anxious to sleep. They were at the junction of the roads, forward to Lousonna and life, sideways to Orba and danger, backwards to Aventicum and death. "Grace, Hermes," he prayed, although he was not a religious man, "let there be a rescue"; and he thought of the kid that he would sacrifice if he ever returned to Verona. Yet today their peril was such as to pass beyond habitual ceremonies. He was no priest, but he knew that part of the secret was the ability to change; not to forget, but to be aware that no moment was ever the same as its fellow. Sometimes there seemed to be no choice; some instinct had driven him to Aventicum, and had held him there against his reason. Was this part of a pattern whose design no living man might know? The stream flowed, the willows rustled, the light breeze was master of the heavy apples; empires, like man, were mortal. In time, Hermes would lead him also to forgetfulness. How he would miss the markets, Demetrius thought; he remembered Gallio riding away (how lucky the fellow had been!) and the old peasant woman who had thrust a bunch of those strong-smelling, white daisies to his nostrils.

A pebble rolled along the slope, and Demetrius sat upright. It was merely a stone dislodged by a mule, and he flopped down again, furious with himself for being unable to sleep. At such a moment why question whether this man or that were alive? The important thing was to rest, so that he would be fresh to continue the journey. He heaved himself into another hollow, only to find a ridge jabbing both shoulders; he slid back into his original position, yawned, and for very restlessness sat up again. This time he heard footsteps.

It was Felix. He had offered to remain with Rufus, hidden near the main road, so that they could warn the others if soldiers passed them.

"Well, what news?" the trader asked, as Felix sat down at his feet.

"We saw the young officer who warned us yesterday evening."

"The man who had had fever?"

"Yes, he had got a pony, and there was another soldier with him. They came towards us slowly, the animals were tired. I was afraid that he might recognize my face, so I whispered to Rufus who he was, and left him to do the talking."

"And what did the officer say?"

"He would not have spoken to a peasant, but Rufus saluted and gave the number of his former legion. The officer said they were returning to Lousonna, because they both belonged to its garrison, and that he pitied anyone left in Aventicum; the city was doomed."

"Did he tell you anything more?" Thallus asked. He had evidently not been sleeping quite so soundly as they had supposed.

"The streets had been quiet this morning, and the day just as hot, but it is lucky that we got away last night. From the first watch there was an order that nobody was to leave the town. He had permission to go only because he was rejoining his post."

They looked at each other. "The gods are merciful," Demetrius said, remembering the market again, and an old poplar that had grown to a surprising height above a neglected garden.

"He ordered Rufus to join him, so Rufus pretended that he was waiting for his son, whom he had sent to a well, and that they would follow as soon as the boy got back. Then the officer said that it had been strange to watch the women drawing water from the fountains; he thought that the citizens did not understand what had happened."

"Understand! That is the epitaph for the town,"

Thallus groaned, "and the last report that we shall hear, before it is ashes."

"If only they had taken the money that was wasted on the Games for weapons," Demetrius grumbled.

"My master knew that we needed reinforcements," Thallus answered bitterly, "but he was stubborn. There was a peace party in the city, and it wanted to negotiate with the enemy. You must have met their leader, Modestus; he had the big warehouse on the outskirts, near the amphitheater."

"A fellow like a pole, with a tattered, grey cloak?"

"Yes, he felt the cold, but he was intelligent. He wanted to buy protection from the tribes, and I think that he was right. Then we should all be sleeping in our own beds this evening. Vinodius believed that if he kept the citizens happy, they would not go round shouting, 'We want peace!' Now you see what has happened."

"If you had paid tribute," Demetrius answered firmly, "it would have gained you a year. I know the tribes. Once they see silver, they also smell plunder. Nothing will hold them back except a strong arm, a wide shield and a sharp sword."

Nobody replied; they sat in a half-circle looking at the water, and Demetrius wondered why men clung so firmly to the impressions of their youth. Thallus could say what he liked: philosophers made indifferent statesmen. The barbarians had no scruples; they had to be met by force, not rhetoric. All a man could pray for was

179

experience. It was Fortune's gift, and it depended upon opportunity, not treasure. The acrobat in the square was more likely to escape from this tumult than the steward; once thought was separated from human passions, it turned so easily to a poison. "I hope Nennius got through," he said at last. There was a glow of red along the sky, but it would soon be dark.

"Listen!" Felix said. They could hear the strong, regular footsteps of the trained legionary, coming nearer and nearer up the path. Rufus looked anxious as he swung into view. There was a dirty, frightened urchin at his heels. "This child escaped when some ox carts were plundered two or three miles up the road. The attackers came from the hills."

"They must have gone in the opposite direction, so even if they were Alemanni, we are still safe, because they would be moving back towards their army at Aventicum. The question is, did they sack Orba first?"

They stared at each other, and instinctively Demetrius caught up his cloak; he felt suddenly cold.

Nobody spoke, then Thallus almost whispered, "Could they have been local thieves?"

"Even so, they may have caught Nennius on his way up; and as the farmers made no resistance, they will certainly attack the road again tomorrow."

"Another messenger must go to Orba," Thallus said decisively.

"But we do not know the way," the trader objected;

"it would be certain death to send a man up an unfamiliar path tonight."

"Could we ride now to Lousonna?"

"We are much too exhausted," Felix interrupted, "besides, think of the noise we should make, dragging some weary mule out of a ditch. It would bring every bandit in the district down on us."

"Then there is nothing else to do," Demetrius said firmly, "but to trust to the gods. I shall offer a second kid, if I see the gates of Verona again." How he wished that he had not cheated at the general sacrifice. Why had he not added the beast that he had vowed after Saltus? This time he was in earnest, and he would buy the two best animals that he could afford.

"Do you suppose you can bribe the heavens with fat meat?" Felix sneered. "Trust in the true God and pray Him to be merciful."

"We must try to accept our fate," Thallus managed to utter, "there will be no suffering once we are dead."

Felix took off his cap, bent down, and splashed some water on his face. He tightened his sandals, while they stared at him. "I think I remember the way," he said, "I noticed it when I came down. Domina Julia was kind to me when I had that fever. I had been going to ask you to allow me a day on our return, so that I could take a gift to her."

"A gift!" Demetrius gasped incredulously.

"Yes, she wanted a silver-leafed basil; it grows on the

other side of Aventicum. I shall leave my cloak with you, to travel as light as possible."

"No, Felix," Demetrius scrambled to his feet, "you are the best overseer that I ever had. You will never find the way in the dark. You will stumble over a precipice, even if the enemy does not hear you. It is madness; I forbid you to go."

Felix thrust his cap back on his head, so firmly that it perched on his thick hair like a crown. "I am free," he said proudly, "and God will be with me. I do not have to offer kids, nor pretend to be indifferent when I am trembling all over. Happiness is to come for me, I have never had it on earth." He pushed past his astonished companions, and started wearily up the hill. A mule lifted its head from some thistles, a clod of earth splashed into the stream. "Do not wait for me if the garrison arrives, and I have not returned," Felix shouted, then he waved and turned the corner, out of sight.

"Your overseer may be a good man, and he is possibly saving our lives," Thallus commented with some asperity, "but can you explain why these Christians think it virtuous to be rude? I leave every man to his opinions. If we must die," and he managed a faint smile, "let it be with beauty and detachment."

In a land renowned for sunsets, it was an extraordinary evening, not violent, not fiery, but massed gold and green, as if the inside colour of the ripening grapes had crept into the sky. Everything suggested peace. The woods were violet along the horizon, the last few roses climbed about the balustrade. This dusk differed from a thousand others only because no smoke rose above the cottage roofs, and there were no goats scrambling up the path to be milked.

"We are alone," Valerius said, and Veria felt his arm tighten across her shoulders.

"Quite alone." She had utterly failed to break his stubborn determination to die, simply because that drunken fool in Aventicum had forgotten to send them orders to withdraw; though what good the sacrifice would be to Rome she could not imagine.

"You may stay with me till it grows dark. Then I am sending you to Marcus."

"I shall remain here; Domina Julia is staying."

"I cannot abandon my post without orders," Valerius pleaded helplessly, "but you and my sister and the women must leave."

"Domina Julia is as Roman as you are," Veria kicked a pebble savagely against the chipped wall. "I expect she is oiling the lock that will be battered to pieces in a few hours. She could help these people who have lost their homes, and make herself and Marcus happy; but no, she is a citizen and cannot give up a foot of what she calls Roman ground."

"You are not a soldier, so you do not understand. I have to hold Orba, unless other orders reach me."

"They have probably sent you orders, but the messenger has been killed on the way. Be Helvetian for once, and listen to reason."

A final wagon jolted out of sight, where the white ribbon of dusty road climbed a crest of rising ground. The outlines of the distant and tremendous mountains were quite clear. Mortals could not climb such rock; the gods kept such snow free from the desecration and the conflict that human feet brought with them. "It grows thinner around us," Valerius said, and she knew that he had forgotten her. He wanted Veria to sit quietly beside him while he counted his memories over with a miser's fingers, but her senses were stinging with anger and fear. He would die, they would die, because of a law that was blunter than the letters on a broken tombstone, while all the time Marcus was crying out for soldiers to help him hold the valley, and every suggestion that she made was described as "Helvetian indiscipline."

When Fabula had come down the path on that final day, she had seemed to be looking for him. Valerius had been proud of the welcome in what he called her "oceanic" eyes, being never sure if they were wave-blue or river-green: they changed as he looked at them. He had scolded her for being late, and had pretended that some immortal had tried to capture her by throwing honey over her shoulders; they were so fair against his own rust-red skin, burnt as all swimmers were by the sun and lake. "The willows will be cool," she had replied, and he had flung a cloak over the short, soft grass. It matched the emerald at her breast.

Women were all the same, Valerius thought; he could no more count his loves, before or after Fabula, than he could count the petals of these roses. Then what was the mystery that still made her seem the reason for his having been born? He lifted his hand to feel the grapes overhead, he looked at the tendrils; each of his senses was alive and resented death, yet just as certainly as he felt that the enemy was assembling at Saltus, so he knew that he had run his race and left the palaestra, that everything other than that single July was of less importance to him than a game.

Why? Why? Why? And Fabula had been unfaithful to him! Not with a comrade, but with herself. The experience of love had been as passionate a fulfillment as he had known, once they had seemed to dissolve into those particles of light that were a philosopher's plaything or the atoms of a universe. Yet she had never seemed to be aware that such moments were themselves solutions; she was always looking for something more. . . . "I am only a substitute for an immortal," he had grumbled, "are you the bride of the sun-god?" Before she could answer, they had heard voices, he had dived into the lake, and had never seen her again, except once from a great distance, over the heads of people, as she was borne, in apparent unawareness of his presence and in utter tranquillity, towards the temple on her litter.

Valerius was equally oblivious now of the child beside

him who had put a cold hand upon his burning arm in an attempt to prepare herself for the noise, confusion and horror of the night. If only she could stop herself from thinking of a rabbit that she had seen—and Veria shivered—pinned to the ground by an arrow, with a terrible look of pain and helplessness in its film-glazed but still conscious eyes. Yet perhaps it was better this way; she had had her happiness crushed into a handful of days, and would die before it could be lost. It was then, as hope had almost gone, that they heard the sound of panting, and footsteps on the steep path below them. Somebody was struggling up, stopping, breathing, and running forward again. Veria was the first to recognize the boy. "Nennius!" she shouted, "Nennius! What has happened?"

Nennius saluted, the new way that Rufus had taught him, but he looked so tattered in his journey-stained tunic that Valerius smiled. He held out a tablet and gasped, "I was sent because I knew the way," and they saw that it was stamped with the official seal.

Twenty years seemed to drop from Valerius in a moment; he was the eager centurion again of his early days in the army. "You were wrong, Veria; Vinodius has remembered us. We are to escort that ruffian Demetrius to Pennilocus. The governor's scribe is with him. They are transporting some archives on the trader's mules."

"They will be at the crossroads," Nennius gasped. "Raurica has fallen."

"We heard that rumour this morning," Veria said eagerly, "but we did not know if it was true. The village is empty; everybody has left."

Valerius looked at the familiar hills and wondered, for a brief moment, whether Fabula were alive, and if so, where she might be. Then he shouted in his parade voice, "Run, Veria, and warn my sister. We must be out of here within the hour. Get yourself some food, Nennius. I will sound the alarm."

Julia rubbed more sand upon the lip of the cauldron. Five other cooking pots stood on the shelf above her shoulders, as burnished as if they were new. It was foolish to spend her last hours on earth scrubbing the kitchen, but some impulse drove her to polish everything in sight, as if they were waiting, not for attack, but for transfer to another post; and duty required her to be sure that there was no speck of dust in the corners. She had even washed her summer tunics that morning, and hung them on a line to dry.

They had talked about invasion for years. It had come, and she was just as unprepared as the most indifferent of her neighbours. Yesterday had followed the pattern of so many seasons: they had baked bread, watered the beans, and speculated as to when Nennius would return from the city. She had felt a wonderful calmness all day, as if her desire for contemplation were about to be granted to her; when Veria had followed her brother up the hill, she had watched them leave with complete indifference. All turbulence had ceased. She had gone to the wood at dusk to sit beside the statue without thinking at all, except to wonder idly whether autumn would be early after so hot a summer because she had discovered two long, golden leaves lying at her feet in the grass.

Just after the light had come that morning, one of the women had wakened her. "Domina Julia! Domina Julia! Something has happened, the village is empty." She had run to her brother, who had turned out the guard. Two hours later he had returned from a search of the neighbourhood, and had ordered the women to Pennilocus. "They say that Raurica has fallen," he had added uneasily, "it must be merely rumour, but the peasants have fled."

Julia had refused to move, and Valerius, knowing that he could not drive her away by force, had compromised to save his dignity. They were to go at nightfall, and by that time, as they both knew, it would probably be too late. Poor Valerius, he had had so little out of life, yet now, for a second time, he was bringing destruction on his family. If he had taken his discharge when it was due, they could have been safely at Ceresio; or if they had remained at Orba, could have left with the peasants in the morning. Well, she would remain with her brother and the Empire, although the force that was holding them here was something that she could not explain. Perhaps it was simply pride, because as a sacrifice it was useless. At least, she thought grimly, the problem of Marcus was now settled. Julia put the cauldron back on the hearth, and strolled into the courtyard to wash her hands. It was almost time to serve the evening meal. How hot it still was! The water in the basin was as warm as if it had been heated over a fire. She wandered across to the garments that were drying on a line; possibly she could weave a strip to replace that hole where the hem had been ripped by a thorn. To-morrow they must pick more beans . . . clang, the alarm began, she shut her eyes and wondered why her brother was always so foolish, they were throwing their lives away for nothing; then there was a wild, final boom, and the sound of running.

"Domina Julia! Domina Julia!" Veria was panting, but she was also smiling. "Nennius has come with orders for us to escort the archives to Pennilocus. Domina Julia! Where are you?" Then, and she was never allowed to forget this afterwards, Julia heard herself saying, to her own great surprise, "The orders came? And Valerius had no toga on, to receive the messenger? May the gods forgive us."

"All men are to take their weapons, cloaks, and as much food as they can carry," Quintus shouted for the fourth time. The courtyard was crowded. They had led the mule and pony out of the stables, and men were bringing jars of beans and strips of sun-dried meat up from the storerooms. Quintus moved among them, humming a little song, drunk with relief because he had had no intention of remaining at Orba, but had decided that morning to leave with a couple of his comrades, directly it grew dark. Fifteen men could not hold up an army, and to remain at the post to be killed was a waste of men and weapons. Yet he had a deep affection for his commander, and it had grieved him to think of Valerius throwing his life away on account of some mistaken loyalty to that fool at Aventicum. "Careful," he shouted, as some loaves spilled out of a bag, "rope the sacks well, there is a long march ahead of us."

"I have looked at those hills ever since I was a girl," the oldest slave woman chattered, as they helped her to balance herself between two sacks of meal, astride the pony. She had a stiff leg. "To think that at my age I am going to Lousonna."

"Cities are wicked places, mother," one of the soldiers joked. They were all lively after the strain of the day. To fight shield to shield among a hundred comrades was different from listening for enemy footsteps, alone in a wood. "Are you sure you are brave enough to come with us?" another man asked with mock solemnity. "Lousonna is full of thieves."

"Thieves! Afraid! What have I to lose?" She held up the tiny bundle that contained all her possessions, and the onlookers laughed.

"Has anybody seen my second hunting knife," Nennius spluttered, his mouth still full of bread. "I left it in the outhouse."

Veria put a cheese down in front of the man who was packing up the last sack, and beckoned to him. "It's hanging on a nail outside the kitchen; I cleaned it this morning." She picked up a torch from the fire, and they walked over together. "You ran well," she said admiringly, "but you were only just in time."

"Oh, the city won't fall," Nennius seemed very confident, "you should have seen the Guard. They stood in full armour, without moving, on the hottest day this summer, as if they were a temple frieze. But I forgot," he added, with an irritating superiority, "you have never seen a big temple."

"I shall see one soon at Pennilocus. Have you found your knife? They are shouting for us to leave."

"Yes, it's here; it was stupid of you to put it in that dark corner. At least you will see Rufus, as soon as we get to the valley. He knows more about the legions than any man alive. But run, I have to fetch the dogs."

"Assemble!" Valerius came into the middle of the courtyard. He had on armour, and a cloak rolled over his shoulder. The last comers helped each other to fasten their personal bundles on to their backs. "Is everyone here?" Valerius shouted again; his eyes went down the ranks of soldiers—they were now drawn up behind Quintus—until he saw his sister. She was standing beside the pony, with the elderly freedwoman and their four household slaves. Like Veria, she had looped her dress up almost to her knees, and Nennius was next to them, with the two hunting dogs on a leash. "Open the gate," he ordered sharply, "and remember, every third man is to carry a torch."

The bolts had already been drawn, and two men tugged back the heavy doors. Then, as if the years of stagnation had decided to repent and throw a dozen surprises into one evening, a figure marched forward into the glare of the fire. There was a gasp of surprise, as the man said quietly, "Here I am, Domina Julia, it is Felix."

"It may be a trap," Quintus said, half drawing his sword. Felix ignored him, and continued, "My party is waiting at the crossroads. We were afraid that Nennius might not have got through, but I see the boy is here." He had intended to spit at them, "It was not Romans who came to rescue you either," but the soldiers seemed so glad to see him that the bitter words remained unspoken on his lips. He pulled off his cap as Julia came to meet him. "Oh, Felix, you must be exhausted, and you might easily have lost your way on these hills. Valerius, I will give him some food, and we can follow you by the short cut down the steps."

"Do you know where the enemy is?" Valerius asked.

"There was an attack two miles away from us, but it may have been thieves. The peasants are driving their cattle to Lousonna, and the main road will be impassable tomorrow."

"I know the by-paths," Quintus said impatiently, "but the sooner we start the better." Valerius nodded, he gave the signal, and the party began to file, two by two, into the road.

Julia led Felix back into the deserted kitchen. There was a little wine left in the jar that they had opened for supper; she mixed this with water from the fountain, and found some scraps of bread and meat abandoned after their meal. As Felix ate, she glanced guiltily along the row of pots on the shelf. They had taken two of them, and the remaining glass goblet was carefully packed, under her best tunics, in the sack slung over her shoulders; but there were saucers and a cloth still on the table, and every object, even every crumb, seemed to reproach her for leaving them to their fate. The shadows turned into ghostlike figures with wavering fingers (though it was only the fire dying down in the yard) until she shivered. "Do not grieve too much, Domina Julia," Felix pleaded; "I found you the silver-leafed basil; you can start a new garden with it, at Pennilocus."

"Hurry, the others are getting too far ahead." Valerius strode into the kitchen with an anxious face. Without thinking, Julia picked up a common saucer of rough earthenware that she could have bought in any market, and thrust it into a fold of her dress. "Be careful of the loose stones," her brother warned her as they came to the top of the steps, and she nodded.

There was no time for farewell. She looked at the soft, shadowy clump that was her rosemary bush, and felt ivy under her hand as she touched the balustrade. She could not see Quintus, but only lights below her, and the dark, humped outline of the animals. Somebody laughed. Veria was holding a torch up in the air as proudly as if she were going to a festival. The air was warm, and the men were happy; they were marching away from danger. The stream rustled in the distance, a pebble rolled, some small beast or lizard scurried between two boulders; not a head was turned to look back at the deserted courtyard, and only Julia was crying. To her, Orba was home.

"My tunics!" Thallus groaned. They had given up the struggle to sleep, and Rufus had built a tiny fire that was well hidden among the reeds. "And there was my other cornelian ring! I left it at the jeweller; he was resetting it for me."

"Be thankful that you are alive," Demetrius grunted. He wondered where Felix was; a man could lose his way so easily among these criss-cross paths.

"What is life to me now?" Thallus clasped his knees with his hands, and his long neck drooped forward. "In Aventicum everybody respected me."

Demetrius said nothing. If Valerius did not join them, he was wondering whether it would be wiser to abandon the bales, and to try to make their way across the hills.

"If my master had only listened," Thallus continued;

"Modestus had sent a messenger to the chiefs. It was merely a question of the silver that they wanted. The taxes would have been severe, I know . . ."

"But not on you. The tolls fell on us."

"I admit that they were heavy; but life would have continued as before, except that we should all have been a little bit poorer."

"And next year, some other tribe would have marched up to your walls, and demanded a double tribute."

"Vinodius was so obstinate. It was being a soldier, I suppose, and that woman he had. When a woman meddles with a man's affairs, he had better pray for an earthquake to wipe both of them into oblivion."

"No, Thallus," by now Demetrius was thoroughly irritated, "you cannot blame this invasion on women, or youthful insolence, nor set whatever you dislike up as a scarecrow. People have been talking about invasion for the last seven years. We may not know why things happen, but we can learn from the tiny details that surround us. I think you philosophers are too detached; the world may be a shell, as you say, but even slaves have to eat, and find a cloak somewhere when the gales begin. Your tolls and taxes have bled us white, and we are not willing to take the same risks as our fathers. Life is fluidity and change; the barbarians move, but you and your fellows in the Treasury watch our misery with a marble indifference."

"Yet if this is really our last night on earth," Thallus bent down to draw a cloak over Aristo's legs, the child had kicked it aside, "are you thinking of either markets or women? Life must mean more to you than such trifles."

"If I look back," Demetrius answered gravely, "I remember a journey. It was three years ago, and I had gone with one of my men to the foothills south of Verona to see a farmer about a mule. Coming back, we lost our way. It was autumn by the calendar, but summer had relented and returned again, and I was not frightened; we had several hours of daylight left, and we could see our road, like a long, white whiplash, winding down the valley below us. We scrambled down the slopes, through a lot of those purple flowers that the herdsmen grumble about, because if the cows eat them they spoil the milk, when my man was stung by a hornet. Such stings bring fever, so when we met a shepherd, a few moments later, I asked him for help. He pointed out a temple; it was small, and so well hidden that only a native would have known that it was there. We walked up to it, and by that time, my servant's leg was so swollen that we did not need to tell the old priest on the steps what had happened. 'A hornet sting,' he said. 'I must fetch Fabula.'

"We sat down on some stones, and presently two women appeared. One was a peasant, no longer young, and with the olive-coloured skin that is common to that district but that the men in Verona consider too dark to be beautiful. The other was not a woman but a goddess. In my opinion, most of the tales about the gods

196

come out of a poet's head after he has made too many libations, yet looking up at these eyes that seemed able to read, not my thoughts, but something about me that I did not know myself, I almost whispered, 'Have pity on me, Maia!' The body was that of a youth, the skin hardly bronzed, and not lined, yet I knew that I was in the presence of something ancient and timeless, a flower, if you will, from the youth of the world. I knelt, I thought of Hermes who was born of Maia in a shepherd's cave; but before I could speak she said in a voice that turned our ordinary phrases into bird songs, 'I hear your servant has been stung by a hornet. Come to the fountain with me first.'

"We followed her through an orchard that had nine beehives in it, I counted them and was surprised at the number, till we reached a mountain stream. Some of it was flowing into a basin, through a couple of hollow logs. They examined the leg to be sure that the sting was out, bathed it, and rubbed it with salve. The ointment was so powerful that the swelling began to go down almost immediately; I was a fool not to offer to buy some from her, but I was dazed, and seemed to have lost my voice. She gave us some herbs afterwards, steeped in mountain water, that took away our thirst. We went back to the temple for the customary prayers, and I managed to mutter, 'Your price?' She nodded towards a cracked saucer that had been left out for offerings, and I dropped in a whole silver piece. She did not thank me, although they cannot often have seen silver in so remote a spot, but her companion almost shouted her gratitude. Then, as we turned to leave, she smiled; she was standing with her back against a column, and as I passed her, she murmured 'Farewell' to me in my own language! I am still wondering where she learned her Greek. It was Fabula I thought of on our march today: Fabula, a fable, the flower that sends us wandering, and looking for something that we can never find, and I wonder only why it happened to me."

"If you had been scrambling about the hills all day, it was a touch of the sun. I saw a vision myself this afternoon, a waterfall leading to three fountains; each was as precise as the cipher on a slate." Thallus stretched his legs in front of him, felt them, and groaned.

"I should not have wanted to sleep with her. I am mortal enough to prefer things that I understand. But it is useless now dreaming about a Lydian, with half my markets in ruins."

"Aie! It is women, I tell you; why were either of us born?"

The trader shrugged his shoulders, "The first march is always the worst. What's that?" He sprang to his feet as Rufus approached. "I saw a light," the legionary said, "it must be the Orba party, the Alemanni would travel without torches."

It was cool now. The reeds rustled as men scrambled to their feet, some splashed water on their faces, others gathered round the almost extinguished fire. "If Valerius wants to see the archives, show him my bundle," Thallus said, fastening Aristo's cloak with a Gaulish pattern silver brooch. "I brought my two seals, and the annual accounts."

"You brought what?" Demetrius said in surprise. "I saw your pack was heavy, but I thought it was your winter clothes."

"I was not going to let a pack of barbarian wolves destroy my life's work. Even if it meant abandoning some tunics, I took the summary of the taxes, and the grain lists; but I had to leave the day-to-day accounts."

Demetrius shook his head in mingled perplexity and admiration; once Aventicum were destroyed, such documents would lose their value to anybody. Thallus must have guessed his friend's thoughts, because he added, "The rolls represent my life, and I was faithful to my duties. My master knew that I had never accepted a bribe."

Vinodius gave you gifts and they were the equivalent, the trader thought; but he merely said quietly, "I know how this upheaval has upset you, but believe me, Thallus, you have less cause than most of us to fear the future. A dozen men in Verona will be anxious to take you into their service. The youth of today has no head for the imperial ciphers; many of them cannot even write."

Rufus had gone forward to hide near the old barn, so as to warn the trader's party if the men were strangers. "Orba!" They heard his shout echoing down the road, and the answering "Orba" of a score of voices.

"Build up the fire," Demetrius ordered, flinging a handful of dry twigs on to the embers. As it flared up, they saw their friends coming down the slope towards them. Quintus was in front, with the stub of a torch still in his hand; there was Domina Julia with Felix at her side; the helmet crest at the rear belonged certainly to Valerius. "Must I always lose my sleep to come and rescue you?" a soldier shouted. It was the man who had found Demetrius above Saltus. Then everybody began to talk at once; it might have been a hunting party, or the harvest procession to a temple in the hills.

VIII

Aventicum.

PLINIUS yawned. His eyes were strained from staring into the darkness, and the man who was to
relieve him was overdue. He could still hardly believe
that the enemy was almost at the walls. He had been left
an orphan early, and his uncle had threatened him with
the Alemanni since childhood: he must not hunt beyond
Balma, "because of the tribes"; he had to memorize
speeches so as to complete his legal studies, "before we
are attacked." Yet now, if he was to die that day with
an arrow through his chest, what waste the grammar
had been! All that mattered was the lake, the cool grey
water, the patches of hot sand. He was lonely, he missed
Gallio; the fellow had been right after all, he was des-
perate with impatience and discomfort. Why couldn't
men sleep, eat, swim and hunt without ravaging the
woods and killing each other? Nobody wanted war.

He had been stationed on the southern wall, together
with most of the other auxiliaries, in one of the poorer
districts of Aventicum. There were a few gardens below

him, some old, neglected trees, and a small temple that had crumbled into ruins. Outside there were a number of thatched sheds, hardly worth burning, he reflected, and then was ashamed of the thought, whose inhabitants had fled during the previous day. At the corner of the parapet where he was keeping his watch, there was a long, ominous crack in the stones. Nothing had been repaired for years.

Plinius had looked at the fields so long that the blackness seemed to be full of moving forms, yet he was terrified of giving a false alarm, lest the centurion yell at him for a fool, as he had yelled at one of his companions. He yawned again; he was extremely sleepy, it seemed impossible that it was less than twenty-four hours since all men able to bear arms had been summoned to the forum.

It was going to be another perfect day, and he thought regretfully of the swimming party that they had planned. Only a few yards away there was a small gate through which he had passed a thousand times on his way to the river. He wondered where Gallio was; probably by now he had already reached the passes; if he had only taken his friend's advice, they might be sauntering up some wind-blown path together. He still could not believe that Raurica had fallen. It must be that the tribes had swept across the river, as their centurion had said the night before, and that the governor of the fort was waiting until they had dispersed, to attack the Alemanni from the rear. Perhaps, if war had to come, it was better to fight now and have it over. He was tired of Modestus and the peace party, with their groaning and complaints.

What was that? Surely something had moved between the huts whose shapes he could just distinguish in the first light before dawn. There was a deafening yell; a sudden spurt of flame lit the parapet like a torch. The thatched roof below him was ablaze.

Plinius turned to run back to the tower, but at that moment a cloud of smoke drove him back; he could neither see the outposts nor hear the centurion's voice. He began to cough, there was a scream, the sound of a body hurtling from a height, something cracked, and a great stone, almost at his feet, slid into the ditch below him.

Plinius grabbed the balustrade. A mass of tribesmen, their leather shields held high over their heads, were streaming into the city. "Modestus has betrayed us," he shrieked, but his voice was lost in the tumult. Somebody had thrown a brand into some straw, and a raging fire cut him off from his companions. He saw a crest appear at the end of the parapet; he turned and ran, only to meet more of the Alemanni coming up from the opposite side. There was a bough above him, he caught it, heard wood crack but swung himself on to another branch, and from it to a third, before he was able to pull himself up to the temple roof. An arrow whistled over his head, but he flung himself flat on a little ledge, where he was hidden from the enemy by a cloud of smoke and leaves.

Plinius lay there breathless; he felt his eyes close in spite of himself. "Gallio," he murmured; "Gallio"; his friend was the one familiar thing that he had left. He dared not move until the enemy had cleared the wall; they had probably thought that he had fallen to the ground; because they had stopped shooting and were moving, he judged from the sounds, towards the corner of the ramparts.

In spite of the discomfort he must have slept for a moment, because it was broad daylight when he opened his eyes. The thatch had burnt itself out, but apart from some men on the tower he seemed to be alone. He crawled along the ledge, keeping well under the shelter of the branches, and looked across at Aventicum.

There were fires everywhere; villas were flaming, then there would be a space where leaves still stirred in the wind, and he could even see water splashing out of a fountain. The legionaries were drawn up in front of the Treasury. He recognized Vinodius by his crest, but only half the men were there; the surprise must have been complete. Groups of his companions had been cut off in the various towers, but the Alemanni were attacking them one by one, and overwhelming them through force of numbers. There were bodies lying in the roads, he saw a woman clinging to a roof; there were plenty of the leather shields belonging to the enemy, lying among the gardens. The legionaries will hold them, Plinius thought; then he looked from the small company in its shining armour to the great brown mass marching up towards the steps, and knew they were doomed. It was the shell of a racing chariot caught in the mud of a torrent.

They dared not throw their spears, there were too few of them. Plinius choked with horror as the Alemanni stopped, just out of range. Vinodius raised his hand, the men began to move, they were going to try to cut their way through to the forum. Was it a fire behind the Treasury or had somebody undermined the foundations? As the cohort swung forward, there was a roar, the ground shook as if an earthquake had shattered it, and the great wall of the Treasury cracked and fell forward upon the thin line of the advancing Romans. A huge spiral of dust blotted everything from view. Even the ledge to which Plinius was clinging rocked beneath him as he clung to it in terror.

Plinius was so dazed that he stood upright on the parapet; in front and to the left of him there was now nothing but smoke. On his right there was still a garden of untouched green, but once the trees began to burn he would be trapped. Almost without knowing what he was doing, he began to scramble towards the ground, his back against an angle of the wall, his legs outstretched and feeling for toe holds in the ridges of a column. Perhaps there was an army around him, but if so, it was concealed by the fog, and when he reached the courtyard at last, he was apparently alone.

"The gate," Plinius thought, "the gate!" It could not be more than a few yards away. He wrapped his cloak around his mouth and ran forward, pushing his way through the cloudy air as if he were swimming under water. His eyes smarted, he began to cough, but his legs carried him instinctively towards the opening. Modestus or his messengers had done their work silently and well, the ground was trampled into a thick dust, but there was no sign of any struggle, except for one body that had been thrown, apparently, from the parapet above. Looking up, Plinius could distinguish some shapes on the wall itself, but the gate was clear. He raced through, jumped into the ditch, crawled cautiously along it until he came to the path that led to the lake, and then scrambled up between the wreckage of the huts. In an hour the Alemanni would station guards at every corner, but there was still some scattered fighting in the town, and in the confusion half a dozen survivors were running across the fields.

It was strange to stand alive among so much ruin. All Plinius could see of the city were occasional tongues of flame. Somewhere in that desolation, Vinodius and his legionaries were buried under the wall. His uncle's house, the law scrolls and the hunting gear were indistinguishable ash on a burning courtyard. He stood irresolute a moment; ought he to return and die with his friends? Then a boy ran up to him and gasped, "Come, there is still a boat if we can reach the lake in time." It was a fisherman's son, whom he had often helped with the nets. They dashed on across the meadow, trampling down the white, peaceful flowers, while the thunder of falling stones, shrieks and battle cries deafened their ears. "Hurry," Plinius urged, as if he could feel the swirl of the slave whip already curling across his shoulders. They gasped, fixing their eyes on the grasses in front of them; sometimes they slowed to a walk; the noises blurred gradually into a low, continuous moan. A man waved, it was the boy's father. They managed a final spurt; there, under the feathery, overhanging willows, a dozen fishermen were gathered, round a leaky but still serviceable barge.

IX

Pennilocus.

VALERIUS was sitting on a low wall above the
quay, watching men unload the boats. Each ship
had its own gaily painted emblem, and the sacred mark
on the bow. Many citizens from the neighbouring estates
were moving into Pennilocus` for safety; their slaves
struggled ashore bent double under the weight of heavy
sacks, scribes counted boxes, dogs barked, children were
smacked. Yet there was also an air of holiday about the
scene. The water shimmered below him like a thin,
wrinkled tunic; he felt he needed only to press it gently
aside to touch a girl's body underneath, while the ordinary pebbles on the bottom of the lake shone in the sand
like jewels.

There was a special peacefulness in this moment that
he had stolen from the war, that was utterly different
from the earth-born tranquillity of the summers at Orba.
There were no flowers, but the sails replaced them,
white or rust-brown triangles that seemed so luminous
on the horizon, and so stiff when furled along the masts
in front of him. Fifteen years had rolled away, and up

to this instant it had been Pannonia over again, with orders, alarms, the same hours of waiting, and long, unending watches in the darkness. An oarsman sent a wave swirling up to where he sat, and he matched his memories to its ripples. First the crossroads; he had fully realized that Helvetia was doomed only after he had spoken to the governor's steward. The poor fellow had had tears in his eyes while talking of his master. It had seemed wiser to avoid Lousonna, a sprawling circle of villas and gardens built around a port that would be difficult to defend. Instead they had marched for three days across the hills until gorges and broken ground had forced them to descend to the lake. There Marcus had met them (they had sent a messenger ahead) with a company of soldiers. Valerius did not often laugh, but he could not suppress a chuckle of amusement. The man had come up to his sister, who by that time was covered with bramble scratches and burrs, and had said pompously, "I am honoured, Domina Julia, by your unexpected visit, but as you gave me no time to prepare a litter for you, we shall have to return by ship."

A few survivors had struggled in, one or two soldiers and some swift-footed youths. One, Plinius, had recognized the trader. Plinius had seen Vinodius die, and the city go up in flames. Hundreds of the barbarians had been killed, and between these losses and the plunder, their army had halted. There had been no advance upon Lousonna, although armed bands were wandering in the hills, looting cattle and burning villages.

Three or four Helvetians staggered past Valerius with stone for the new defences. "A penny for that!" an old woman shouted indignantly, throwing a fish back into the man's basket. "I wouldn't take it as a gift!" Small boys were hanging nets to dry on wooden frames. Everybody was active, except himself. His soldiers had been absorbed into the garrison, and Quintus was drilling a group of auxiliaries in a narrow field on the other side of the wall. Julia, in spite of her grief, had become a different person since her marriage to Marcus. She had taken over the management not only of the household but of a camp of homeless peasants, as if she had been the mistress of a great establishment since girlhood, and not almost a fugitive herself.

Marcus did not like him. Valerius suspected that his brother-in-law still held him responsible for the family's disgrace and Julia's self-imposed exile. He was to leave the following day (the first fortunate moment to begin a journey since the marriage), with a tablet for the governor of Mediolanum. "He is a friend of mine," Marcus had said briskly, and with the assurance that came not only from being a successful commander, but also from belonging to one of the most distinguished families in the south, "I have asked him to see that the formalities of your discharge are completed as soon as possible, and what is more important, that you get your pension. There will be plenty of civic posts open to you afterwards, either there or at Ceresio." And he had added, as if to soften the blow that he had not suggested retaining Valerius with the legion, "I envy you being able to return to the tranquillity of your own hearth."

In some ways, Valerius was glad himself. It would have been difficult at his age to serve under Marcus, who was as ruthless as he was austere. Was it only character, he wondered, or had landscape its share in the shaping of life? Was sunlit and sleepy Aventicum the partial cause of its governor's indolence, and were these mountains the reason (they were too near and too steep) for his brother-in-law's unceasing vigilance? He looked at the blue haze hovering over the lake, and shrugged his shoulders. In a few more days, there would be nothing left of Helvetia but memories, bitter like the fennel stalks the boys chewed to prove their bravery, sweet as these little grapes.

There was also the problem of Veria. Julia wanted him to marry the child. "She is freeborn, and it would be better for both of you," but that was also because Marcus had commented, "I know that it was difficult on the rim of the frontier, but that girl is more like a goatherd than a woman," with the implication, as Valerius had heard behind the words, that it had been disgraceful to allow Julia to live at Orba at all. "I am a lonely hawk," he had said to his sister afterwards, "and some day Veria may meet a boy of her own age." He had arranged, however, that she should travel with a centurion's wife, who was going with them as far as Mediolanum, and from there to Ceresio, to live with his old cousins who looked after the farm.

"I thought I should find you here." Veria came from behind the nets and sat down beside him, with her legs dangling over the water, almost as if his thoughts had summoned her. In the two weeks since their arrival, the life had gone out of her face and she had become the mere copy of any village girl with a kitchen bowl or a pitcher of water.

"I thought my sister had forbidden you to leave the women's apartment?"

"Domina Julia has taken some coverings to the children who arrived yesterday, and said I could wait here till she returned. I should have come anyhow. I want to hear you say again that you will take me to Mediolanum."

"I promised to take you with me; how can you doubt the word of a Roman?" Valerius teased.

"Oh, I do doubt it," Veria answered unexpectedly, "you wanted me at Orba, you don't want me here."

"Veria! I am sorry that we have been separated from one another, but this is a camp, and neither Julia nor I can permit you to run about as if you were a slave. Are you so unhappy?"

"If I had to stay here, I should die. Even if you do not want me, let me go to your farm; I cannot breathe in this fortress."

"I do want you," Valerius said, without much conviction. "I only wish we did not have to travel with that rascal of a trader."

"Why do you hate Demetrius so much?" Veria asked;

"since Nennius enlisted, he has been the only person who is kind to me."

One of the boats pulled out slowly; two pairs of oars flashed and dipped, flashed and dipped, while the steersman set the pace with a strange Helvetian chant, as old and as barbaric as the hills. "I said I would take you with me," Valerius murmured almost coldly, "but I am afraid you will be lonely at Ceresio." He wanted to be free.

"With you, never."

The Greek had undoubtedly saved their lives, Valerius knew, but it was possible to be grateful to a man and yet dislike him. He despised all traders. The ridge of rock that was just visible in the distance must be directly opposite Orba. He wondered what had happened to the terrace, and if the ivy had been scorched from the familiar walls? Poor child, he patted Veria's arm, all her environment had been completely lost.

"If you promise to take me with you, not because you are a Roman, but because there was a moment when you needed me, I can tell you something. . . ."

"Many promises mean broken promises, but you know I will not leave you here," he answered, smiling and expecting some childlike declaration of love.

"The man you hate so much can answer your question," the words came out with a rush. "Demetrius saw Fabula."

Marcus had given him a horse as a parting present. It was a valuable gift, although Valerius suspected that he had received it mainly because there was not enough fodder for the animal. Neither was there enough food; much of the harvest had been destroyed. His brother-in-law was ruthless, he had ordered most of the fugitives to go south. "We must get rid of the useless mouths," he had replied to Julia, when she had remonstrated with him; "all Helvetians can stay, of course, and there are vacancies in the auxiliaries for other strong and willing fellows, but there is no place here for jewellers or pampered slaves. Besides, it is kinder to send them now before the snows than to watch them dying of hunger round us throughout the winter."

Ever since dawn, groups with mules or solitary wayfarers had started down the road. Besides merchants like Demetrius and a few Helvetians who, having lost their homes, had decided to try their fortunes in a safer land, there were Gaulish silversmiths with their tools carefully packed into rush baskets, a ragged teacher of rhetoric who was already so poor that the Alemanni could have taken nothing from him but his life, and a bewildered African porter who had escaped when his master had been killed; he had been sent to fetch some litter from a barn, and turning round had seen the hamlet going up in flames behind him. There were even some rootless wanderers from the country fairs. Nobody sang, many of them left unwillingly; some, it was obvious, would die in the mountains. Marcus was sending an escort with them to the foot of the pass, ostensibly as guard but really to see that no more farms were plundered, and he had even arranged to give a meagre ration to those completely without funds. It was an act of kingly generosity, because it would be difficult, with the utmost thrift, to feed the garrison until the following spring.

It was still summer, though it was a fortnight later than the traders usually left. The peasants were on the slopes, picking fruit, cutting extra grass, or tending the cows. The rocks above them were so clear that they seemed porous in the light, and there was no trace of snow upon the highest of the peaks. Things ended, and yet were continuous, Valerius thought, gathering up the slack of the reins; he knew every blade of grass in the now desecrated Orba, and yet he was returning to a home that would be as strange, after these many years, as this unknown and golden valley. He wondered if he would ever see Julia again? They had been insistent that he must come back to visit them one summer, after the barbarians had been driven once more across the Rhine. Marcus had hinted that in another year or so he might be transferred to Brixia or Bergomum, but even so their companionship, even their quarrelling, had ended. Julia was already a stranger. "Veria," he called; she was riding his old pony, a few paces behind him. "Veria, are you sad to have left your playmate behind?"

"That was what Nennius was, a playmate. We both knew that when the moment came, we should separate from each other. He always wanted to be a legionary, and, besides, now he has Rufus to look after him."

"My brother-in-law knows a good soldier when he sees one," Valerius grunted, as they trotted past a pedlar and his boy, with a big basket of earthenware lamps swinging from a pole balanced on their shoulders. Marcus had immediately offered the harness maker a room and rations if he would remain with the garrison. "I went to say farewell to Rufus last night, and he was so busy mending a corselet that he had hardly time to wish me a safe journey."

"It is Demetrius who is sad; in spite of all his grumbles, he liked Felix."

"Julia always gets her own way in the end," Valerius sighed. It had amused even Marcus to watch "surly Felix" guarding his adopted mistress as if he were a rough and awkward watchdog. "Both of them believe in their own religions so firmly," he continued, "that I should have supposed that they would quarrel. But no, they stick to each other like glue." It was reassuring, all the same, to know that his sister would have the freedman near her if Marcus later became absorbed by his ambitions and there was fresh danger from the tribes. The basil that had been planted in the new garden with so much ceremony was the first present that Felix had brought to anyone during his life.

Yet they are both harsh, Veria thought, drawing abreast of Valerius on the now empty road. "You cannot imagine how happy I am to leave that horrible city.

It bewitched you. Here, in the country, you like me again."

"I always liked you."

"You forgot me at Pennilocus. It was as if you had never heard my name. If you had left me behind, I should have jumped into the lake. I know you are returning to Fabula, but there will be air on your farm, and they will not talk to me about the duties of a Roman matron." And I can have my memories, Veria thought, without Domina Julia to sneer at them.

"Barbarian! But you need not be afraid of Fabula now." Why had she wasted her beauty in that desolate temple, Valerius wondered; her family was powerful, she ought to have married again. "I made, my peace with Demetrius," he added, "and do you know what he gave me?"

"Oh, the fur cloak." Veria shrugged her shoulders, as if the gift were without importance. "He loved her too in his way, though I can understand that he would rather live with a Lydian; and because she liked you, he wanted you to have it."

"It is most unsuitable," Valerius said sternly.

"You can wear it when you ride to visit her," Veria said maliciously, kicking her pony with her heel so that it bounded in front of him.

A girl came running out of the vineyards and waited for them to pass. A hawk rose, on his right hand, above dark cliffs. He wanted Veria to be happy. It had been a shattering blow for them all to be torn from their

217

familiar dwelling and flung into the midst of strangers. Later on, in the south, she might change, or perhaps, once his mind was quiet again, he could accept Julia's solution of a marriage. He had an uneasy feeling that he was going to miss his sister. The child was not Fabula, but she would let him dream in peace.

"Suppose I found that temple; she might not remember me," he suggested.

"She would remember you," Veria answered firmly.

"You need not be afraid," Valerius repeated again. "You shall stay with me at Ceresio, unless you want to leave yourself. And now, look! There is Demetrius and that absurd friend of his, waiting for us at that thicket. Once we join them, you must ride modestly with the centurion's wife until we reach our destination. I insist upon the traditions being respected. After we are at my farm, you can run as wild as you like."

Valerius could not see the lake as he turned for a final farewell, but only the thin, white columns where the fishermen dedicated their nets. Marcus and Julia had long since gone about their daily occupations; curiously enough, he felt no sense of loss, but only as if Fate had lifted up two broken slabs and joined them together again. He had expected age to come to him imperceptibly, with the hills turning from green to white, and white to green, as summer followed winter. Now the invasion was driving him home. Creation sprang from eternity, but it also was transient; no second experience was exactly like the first. "We all ask to be happy," he said, "but it happens to us rarely, one or two moments in a lifetime."

"This is one of them," Veria answered, transformed again into the wild creature that he had known in the woods. "I wish there were no centurion's wife, and that we could ride to Mediolanum alone."

The fields were gold. The grapes were the colour of sunlight and the soon-to-fall leaves. There was stubble higher up, tiny, bobbing yellow apples, a marsh with flies and water lilies. Aristo was already waving to them, Thallus and Demetrius were standing beside their mules, a herd of goats was browsing about a cave in the rocks. Happiness? Valerius thought: for him it had been the moment when he had dived, with Fabula approaching him, before he had spoken to her. "I do not know how many years we have left," he muttered, as if speaking to himself; and what did time matter if a man's full experience had begun and ended in a single summer? Yet if this were past, at least he could give what happiness he could to others.

Veria looked up anxiously; was the black depression of last spring about to fall on him again? Then she was reassured. He trotted forward, because she was still a pace ahead of him, and as they drew abreast of one another, he brushed a twig from her pony's mane. "Perhaps the world is a fable," he said. Then, because she looked up at him in bewilderment, he added gently, "The pass is open; and, if the gods will, we shall reach Ceresio and end our lives there together."